CW00434204

Lesbian Threesomes, Sexy Surprises

Sexy Surprises, Volume 12

Giselle Renarde

Published by Giselle Renarde, 2023.

Table of Contents

Lesbian Threesomes, Sexy Surprises

6 Erotic Stories
Giselle Renarde

And Kimi Makes Three

There's a bit of truth in the old joke that lesbian sex is just a quiet cup of tea in a room full of cats.

It doesn't start out that way. I can only speak from experience, but when Jody and I first started dating, it was fire. We were so hot for each other back then. I couldn't keep my hands off her ass or my mouth off her tits. She would spend hours between my legs, licking my clit, thrusting her fingers up my snatch. God, it was amazing.

But that was a long time ago. After eight years together, Jody and I had regular sex, but... I don't want to say it was *boring*. Okay maybe it was, just a little.

That sounds mean, I know. I don't intend it that way. I love Jody more than I've ever loved anyone.

Anyway, one weekend Jody and I checked out the arts and crafts show that's held every summer in our neighbourhood. We didn't need anything, but Jody spotted this vase at a pottery vendor, and she picked it up. Typical lesbian weekend.

It wasn't until we got home that Jody realized the vendor had wrapped her ceramics in one of those free newspapers with all the sex ads in the back: six pages of "Asian Escorts and Massage."

Wow, those photos got my temperature on the rise!

2

Jody and I fell onto the couch so close our thighs touched. We opened the newspaper and ogled page after page of young women in sexy lingerie.

The girls presented themselves in a variety of pin-up poses. Some smiled coyly or hugged their tits. My favourites were the bold ones, the girls who grabbed their firm little breasts and held them up, on display for everyone to see. Breasts always were my weakness. Some of them leaned forward and pouted their lips, so you didn't know whether to stare at their cleavage or their pretty pink mouths.

And, God, those mouths! Every time I blinked, I saw pretty Asian girls between my legs. I wanted them all.

"Do you think these pictures are real?" Jody asked me.

I couldn't speak. My breath was taken away by the sheer beauty of those girls. What was it about them? Their mock-innocence? Their sexy schoolgirl outfits? The bikini tops that rose so high on their tits the fabric scarcely clung to their nipples? I was getting wet just looking at those slutty photos.

The words didn't help. The ads said things like:

100% Horny Playful Asian GFE!
Excellent Service, No Rush, Guaranteed!
Young, Busty, Cute, Anything Goes!
Fun, Friendly, Tight, Juicy!

"Tight and juicy!" Jody read. The words obviously had the same impact on her that they'd had on me. Her eyes sort of glazed over as she read the ads. And then she pointed to a picture of a sweet-faced girl with naked, pendulous breasts.

Her name, according to the paper, was Kimi. There were little stars on the page to disguise her nipples, and she had an open red gingham shirt hanging off her shoulders. I couldn't

3

get over those tits! They couldn't possibly be real, such big breasts on such a little girl.

"Should we?" Jody asked, pointing to the spot where it said: $40 NUDE ORAL.

I wasn't going to pretend I didn't want it. The girls in these ads could get me off any day of the week. I wouldn't hide my desire.

Jody was nervous, so I made the call. It was a cell number and went straight to voicemail, so I left a message. Not a minute later, someone calling herself a "booking agent" phoned back to set up the date. She had a bit of an accent, and I wondered if it was Kimi herself on the phone.

God, those tits—they were all I could think about.

I'd never done this before. I wondered if the girl on the phone would think it was weird that two women were requesting a hooker. Did other lesbians pay for sex? Nobody talked about it, so I assumed it didn't happen.

We set the date for later that evening. I don't think Jody or I could have waited any longer. We would have changed our minds if we'd had to.

We were a bundle of nerves as we waited for Kimi to arrive. I tried catching up on some emails, but I couldn't concentrate. I don't know what Jody was up to. We didn't talk about what might happen. We didn't discuss it at all.

There was a knock at the door, and my spine went arrow-straight. I was sure, absolutely one hundred percent sure, that I was going to have a heart attack.

But I didn't.

I started thinking, "I can't do this, I can't do this..." but even as I thought it, I made my way to the door.

Jody was already there, holding the handle. Just holding it. Just standing there.

I put my hand on hers, and we opened it together.

The girl standing on the other side was pretty as a picture—but *was* she the girl in the picture? Hard to say. Without actually holding the newspaper beside her, I couldn't tell. Maybe once her soft yellow cardigan came off, I'd recognize the tits.

Yes, that's right—our hooker wore a cardigan.

It was cute, actually, with a felt flower pinned to the chest. Her whole outfit reminded me of a 1950's sock-hopper, but with a modern flair. Asian girls had a knack for looking good in quirky outfits. That's something I never could pull off.

When we asked if she was Kimi, the girl nodded demurely. We welcomed her in and she entered, holding her purse and her jacket in front of her. I wondered if she dressed this way for everyone, or if this was something special for the crabby old lesbians. It did make me happy that she wasn't wearing some slutty spandex thing.

"Nude oral?" the girl asked. She held out her hand, and I realized she wanted payment upfront. Then she asked, "One or two?"

I wasn't exactly sure what she meant, but Jody said, "Oh, on both of us. One and then the other."

Kimi smiled as I placed the cash in her hand—ratty, wrinkled twenty-dollar bills with the queen smiling up at us. For the first time ever, I wondered why the Queen of *England* was on Canadian money, and then I chastised myself for thinking about something so irrelevant. There was a prostitute in my living room! I should be... well, I didn't know what I should be doing. Then I started feeling nervous.

I looked to Jody, who smiled at me the way the queen was smiling on the twenty.

My stomach tied itself in knots.

Kimi asked if we were a couple, and Jody responded that we were, but even her voice was trembling now. The girl smiled, and then asked how long we'd been together. It surprised me that she seemed curious about us. I guess I figured we were just money to her, just bodies, but she appeared interested in Jody and I as people, and that really put me at ease.

Her accent was thicker than the girl on the phone, but I could see the enthusiasm in her eyes. She talked about the weather, and about the arts and crafts show—she'd been there as well. Strange to think the girl who was now our hooker had been walking around with the crowds, just one more person.

I guess I'd never thought of prostitutes as real people.

When Kimi asked where we'd like to do it and who wanted to go first, I got nervous again. I felt a little weird about taking my clothes off in front of her. Jody must have felt the same way, because she asked Kimi to strip for us.

In a flash, Kimi's expression went from innocent to saucy. When she grinned, her lip turned up more on one side than the other. That subtle tease made my pussy pound.

Our pretty hooker unbuttoned her cardigan. The tease continued, rendering my legs so wobbly I had to sit down.

Without a bit of shyness, Kimi shrugged off her sweater. That's when I got my first look at her gorgeous tits. The firm cups of her dainty white bra hugged them sweetly. There was just enough lace around her cleavage to shift her lingerie out of the boring zone—not that any garment could truly be boring on a body like hers!

Kimi stepped out of her skirt, giving us a good view of her long, smooth legs. She didn't take off her square heels, and I was glad about that. She reminded me of the naughty librarian who takes the bun out of her hair and becomes a sex goddess.

Bending forward, Kimi grabbed her tits and pressed them together. I couldn't take my eyes off that glorious line of cleavage as she juggled and jiggled her big breasts. God, I wanted to touch myself. I wanted to touch her, too!

"You like my big tits?" Kimi asked as she hypnotized us with the marvellous pair. "You want to touch my big fucking titties?"

"Yeah, yeah." I was panting like a dog as I grabbed her breasts from behind. She sighed, and that sound made me want to come. I missed that enthusiasm for touch, that sensitivity.

She let me strip off her panties, then undo her bra, and when her big boobs tumbled from the cups, I was there to catch them.

I told her to lick Jody's clit. I wanted to hear my woman come while this gorgeous slut ate her cunt.

Jody raced out of her clothes as Kimi sank to the floor in front of the couch. I went with her, riding her back all the way, hugging her small body as I fondled her amazingly supple, soft tits. Her nipples were hard little pebbles between my fingers, and they were all I could think about until I heard Jody gasp.

Draped over Kimi's naked back, I looked up to see her black hair cascading over one shoulder, her face buried between my partner's thighs. I'd gone down on Jody countless times, but for some reason this was a thousand times more exciting.

I watched her lips part. Her mouth opened wide. The sloppy sound of our hooker's wet tongue on my girlfriend's pussy ramped up my arousal so high I released one of Kimi's tits and traced my hand down her back... down her ass crack...

I wasn't sure if I was allowed to do this. Kimi seemed to trust us as much as we were trusting her, so I took a chance and found her with my fingers. The newspaper ad was right—she was incredibly tight, and so wet her juice was dripping down between her legs.

Jody's eyes fluttered closed as Kimi lapped her clit. Our living room filled with body sounds—the wet squelching of my fingers plunging in and out of Kimi's cunt, the sweet lapping of Kimi's tongue on my woman's clit, and our whimpering, moaning, sighing, grunting. We were all so turned on. Three women, just a big ball of juicy female arousal!

I was so jealous of those two, because they'd been smart enough to take off their clothes early on. Me, I was still fully dressed and wishing my clothing would just melt off my skin. It felt so damn good to have half my hand shoved up Kimi's snatch while she went at Jody's cunt with her mouth.

Jody was kicking and screaming now, loving every moment of our Kimi's tongue teasing her clit. I wanted to watch. I wanted to see Kimi's face buried between my lover's thighs, licking and flicking, sucking that sweet bud like a little cock.

The cravings rose up in me, but I couldn't decide. Did I want to lick or be licked? Suck or be sucked? But then I remembered what I'd paid for, and I figured I might as well get my money's worth.

Tearing out of my clothes, I threw myself beside Jody on the couch. Kimi moved from Jody's pussy to mine, like a baby shifting from one breast to the other. Everything felt otherworldly, like a dream. Real life was never this good, never this easy. I had a gorgeous young woman between my legs, naked, with the biggest damn tits I'd ever seen up close and personal, and what did it take to get her there? Nothing, really. Just a little phone call, just a little cash. It was too good to be true.

Sliding two long fingers into my pussy, Kimi rubbed my g-spot enough to warm my whole pelvis. I couldn't believe how close I was to orgasm already. All the watching and waiting had turned me on like crazy, and I knew the moment her tongue met my clit I was going to blow.

I watched her pretty face as she drew in close. She kissed my clit, so gentle, so sweet, like a butterfly landing briefly on my skin and then taking right off again. She looked up at me and smiled, but I growled back at her. I wasn't angry or anything, I was just so aroused I couldn't control myself. At all! Grabbing her by the hair, I shoved my slick pussy against her face, which was already soaked with Jody's juice. I rubbed off on her mouth while she squirmed and squealed.

I know I said things to her while my body worked itself into a frenzy of orgasm. "Yeah, you like that, huh? You love the taste of my hot fucking cunt, don't you?" Stuff like that. Stuff I never said to Jody.

Kimi just kept nodding, gulping, gasping, saying, "Uh-huh! Uh-huh!"

The look in her eyes put me over the top. She was scared or something. Cautious, maybe, like she was trying to gauge if I was a danger to her.

I wasn't, of course. I wasn't a danger to anyone, but I scoured my pussy against Kimi's beautiful face until I'd come in crashing waves, over and over, and I couldn't take any more pleasure. Then she backed away, fixing her hair and smiling guardedly between Jody and me.

We thanked her and she thanked us, kneeling on the floor like some kind of sexual servant. After she'd gone, my woman and I sat naked on the couch holding hands for literally hours. In all that time, I kept looking down and expecting to see Kimi there like a toy poodle, wanting to serve us, wanting to bring us happiness and contentment. I hope she knows what she did for Jody and me, because that girl revived us. She really did.

Thank you Kimi, wherever you are.

Kathryn's Kinky

E lementary Days
Kathryn ran down the sidewalk super-fast. Her blonde pigtails waved in the summer breeze like streamers on a bicycle.

Melanie chewed the wet tips of her hair while she watched her best friend's body in motion.

Clinging to her jump rope, Melanie smiled.

When Kathryn arrived at the corner, she halted next to the big red STOP sign. Turning on a dime, she yelled, "What should I do now?"

"Twenty jumping jacks!" Melanie shouted. "I command thee!"

In her mauve corduroy trousers and hand-knitted cardigan, Kathryn hopped on the spot, waving her hands over her head. The girls counted together, loudly, until Melanie's mother popped her head out the front door. "What's all this racket? You'll wake the dead!"

"Kathryn is my slave," Melanie told her mother. "She has to do everything I say."

Melanie trapped her jump rope under her running shoe and pulled on the handles. Her mother didn't seem amused, so she looked away. She looked at Kathryn.

THESE DAYS

Pasha brought last week's mail to the breakfast table and set it beside Melanie's coffee cup.

"You'd better hope there are no overdue bills in there," Pasha said from behind a smile and a lingering accent. "No joy for you if there are late charges."

"Pay the bills late? *Moi?* Never!" Melanie sorted through letters until she spotted her mother's handwriting. Her heart beat a little more cautiously as she plucked the small envelope from the stack. "What's my mom sending us?"

Draining her glass of orange juice, Pasha watched as Melanie opened it. "Looks like an invitation, that little thing."

It *was* an invitation, accompanied by a note from her mother.

"What is it?" Pasha asked, turning to read the card. "A reunion?"

"An elementary school reunion. I didn't know there was any such thing." Melanie skimmed her mother's explanation: the invite had been sent to Melanie's last known address, and Mom had "accidentally" opened the envelope before sending it on.

"You and your *partner* are welcome to stay at the house, if you decide to come," Melanie read. "And I hope you will. It's been such a long time since we last saw you."

"That is sweet. Sounds like an authentic offer."

How could Melanie argue? It did sound authentic, maybe even heartfelt.

"*Your partner*," Melanie muttered. "Makes it sound like we're in business together."

Pasha poured herself more coffee and drank it black. She didn't need to say anything.

"Guess I'd better get packing," Melanie said.

Pasha winked. "I command thee."

She'd heard all the stories.

ELEMENTARY DAYS, REVISITED

"Divorced," Kathryn said. "Twice."

"Ah, yes!" Pasha clapped her hands. "I tried marriage once, to a man. Not my style."

Kathryn beamed a bright white smile. The braces had obviously paid off. Her teeth were beautiful. But, then, Kathryn had beautiful *everything*. Even the drugstore earrings hanging from her tiny lobes looked gorgeous.

It helped that she was the only person in the entire gymnasium who didn't classify lesbians with lepers.

"You two make a cute couple," Kathryn said. "How long have you been together?"

Melanie looked to Pasha for confirmation. "Seven years?" She wasn't really keeping track.

With a nod, Pasha confirmed Melanie's answer. "Seven years this woman has been my friend and lover. *And* my submissive."

The urge to smack Pasha rolled down Melanie's arms and tingled in her fingers, but she forced herself to resist. That's not the kind of thing you go around saying! It was personal. It wasn't anybody's business but their own.

Still, it was Pasha's prerogative to humiliate Melanie in public, in little ways, ways Melanie couldn't really argue with.

Pasha constantly pushed Melanie's limits. That was a good thing, as far as she was concerned. The stretch hurt sometimes, but it was like growing pains: if you wanted to be a bigger person, you had to feel the strain.

"What's a submissive?" Kathryn wanted to know. Nobody was nearby, but she lowered her voice before asking, "Is that a lesbian thing?"

Pasha's eyes glinted. "Not exclusively." Adjusting the folds of her wrap across the folds of her flesh, Pasha said, "You, my dear Kathryn, know far more than you realize."

Melanie looked over her shoulder at former classmates gazing in their direction. Strange to think those greying, balding men had once been boys. And she'd grown up alongside them.

Turning her attention to her plastic glass of boxed chardonnay, Melanie said, "Come on, Pash, you're embarrassing me."

It felt strange, drinking alcohol in the gymnasium. Oh so many after-school volleyball tournaments had been played here. Kathryn was always first string. Melanie had been a sub—*even then*, she mused.

Maybe that's where it all began.

With a silent chuckle, Melanie took a sip of wine. Setting her plastic glass on the table, she said, "Let's get out of here."

Pasha and Kathryn turned to her with puzzled brows. Kathryn was still cheerleader-blonde, stylish and skinny. Pasha was heavy-set, with dark hair that ventured unapologetically down her cheeks and even across her lip. It formed a moustache in the right light.

"Get out of here why?" Pasha asked, gesturing around the room. "We have only just arrived."

That wasn't entirely true. Melanie had chatted with a few of her teachers from back in the day. They seemed old, but not different. Strangely, her age-mates seemed *different*, but not *old*. As a child she'd enjoyed spending time with her peers, but people changed a lot between the ages of eight and thirty-eight.

Leaning across the table, Kathryn childishly chewed her middle finger. "I have a hotel room," she said.

That statement ought to have been shocking, but Melanie wasn't surprised in the least. In tucked-away corners of society, the label "lesbian" seemed to smoke all the bi-curious bees out of the hive and drive them straight to the honey pot.

Besides, this was Kathryn. They hadn't seen one another since they were fourteen years old, when Kathryn's family moved to Alberta. Even then, it was unspoken, but... there was *something*.

Pasha clapped her hands slowly in front of her face. "Kathryn, my dear Kathryn!" Setting her hand on the girl's bare forearm, Pasha gushed, "We accept your kind invitation for an evening of boundless debauchery."

For a long moment, Kathryn didn't flinch.

Then, bending down, she grabbed her purse from the floor. She fixed up her lipstick before rising to her feet. After she'd smoothed her tight white dress against her thighs like a Milan model, her catwalk-cool expression broke.

"This is nuts," Kathryn said, with a glittering giggle. Blonde waves danced against her naked shoulders when she shrugged. "So, let's go. Now or never."

As Pasha leaned against the table, she offered Kathryn a generous smile. "Now or never."

HOTEL BATHROOMS

Pasha wouldn't let Melanie drive when she'd had a drink, even if she'd only taken one sip. As they all packed into the car—Kathryn in the passenger seat and Melanie in the back—Pasha joked about being the world's only teetotal Russian.

Kathryn chuckled politely.

Melanie had heard that one a hundred times before. She leaned against the car door.

Could Kathryn ever replace her as Pasha's favourite? Pangs of jealousy flitted across her scalp and singed her hair before escaping into the ether. Silly notion.

When they arrived at the hotel parking lot, Pasha took her empty water bottle out of the cup holder. She turned to look Melanie straight in the eye. "I will bring this, yes?"

A lot of Pasha's statements sounded like questions, but they weren't questions.

Kathryn looked from the water bottle to Melanie, and then to Pasha. "I have bottled water in the room—it's in the mini-fridge."

With a throaty chuckle, Pasha said, "My dear Kathryn, you do not want to hand me a bottle of *cold* water."

Kathryn obviously didn't understand.

Melanie did.

Maybe their collective body heat had raised the temperature inside the car, because the mango scent of the dashboard air freshener seemed stronger than ever. It seeped into Melanie's body and filled her head. She would need to keep that pleasant aroma with her, at least in her mind. It would counteract the putrid odour Pasha would soon compel her to extract from beautiful Kathryn.

As soon as they'd entered Kathryn's hotel room, Pasha asked to use the bathroom. Big surprise. Melanie knew exactly what Pasha was planning. It behoved her to anticipate her Domme's every thought and desire, but Kathryn, poor dear Kathryn, obviously didn't have a clue what she would soon be subjected to.

The hotel bed was a mess of pantsuits and dresses.

"I didn't know what to wear," Kathryn explained as she sheepishly picked up.

Melanie watched Kathryn's white pumps step, step, step—crossing from bed to closet, closet to bed. Kathryn's bare legs gleamed like they'd been waxed recently and polished with oil. Her dress was so tight it rode up her thighs as she walked. She stopped every so often to pull down on the hem.

What a body!

Kathryn's abs appeared defined under her white spandex dress. Her tits spilled out the top, barely concealed by the noticeable white bra underneath. Melanie kept waiting for her old friend to bend the wrong way so she could catch a glimpse of a rosy nipple.

Maybe Kathryn was the reason all those guys at the reunion were staring at their table—it wasn't about "the lesbians" at all.

Her old friend had certainly kept fit for something. Or someone. Her ex-husband, no doubt. Kathryn had mentioned she'd sensed he was cheating before she knew it for sure. Maybe she started working out for him, in hopes he'd stay.

Sad...

"What did Pasha mean?" Kathryn asked in a hush. "She said I know more than I realize about the submissive thing. What was she talking about?"

"Oh."

Now Melanie felt sheepish. She didn't like introducing the concept to those who didn't know much about their ways. Some people had a hard time understanding.

Or maybe Melanie wasn't very good at explaining herself. She knew in her heart what Pasha meant to her, but she could never get the words out.

"I told Pasha the stories of when we were kids," Melanie said. "How you always wanted me to tell you what to do."

A strange smile bled across Kathryn's lips.

"I gave commands and you carried them out: tie my shoes, eat a piece of liver, put that traffic cone on your head. Remember that? When we were really young, I mean."

With a chuckle, Kathryn said, "Oh, yeah. That was stupid. I don't know why I was like that. I didn't want to make decisions, I guess."

Melanie sat on the edge of the bed. "It's not stupid."

The bathroom door opened with a squeak and Pasha called, "Come here, my dears."

Sliding off the mattress, Melanie walked directly to her Domme and sensed Kathryn following behind.

"She is going to leave that dress on," Pasha instructed.

Melanie offered a subtle nod and entered the bathroom. It was wonderfully large and sparkling white, in true hotel fashion.

Pasha had pulled back the shower curtain. Her water bottle rested on the clean marble counter. It was full now, and the nozzle-lid was back on top. Pasha handed it to Melanie while Kathryn stood in the threshold. It was warm. Not hot, but warm.

"Come inside," Melanie said.

She never knew *how* she knew what Pasha desired. The expectations were inside her. For Melanie, being a true submissive meant anticipating Pasha's needs and wishes, and acting on them without direction.

Tonight Melanie would clean out Kathryn and eat her ass.

All for Pasha.

Kathryn took a single step into the bathroom, and then paused. Her gaze betrayed nothing. She didn't even seem confused.

Could she possibly know what was coming? She seemed so innocent.

Watching the water bottle, Kathryn asked, "What should I do now?"

Pasha leaned against the counter. It was very rare that she gave Melanie instructions anymore. Melanie knew what to do.

Pointing at the pristine bath mat lying across the rim of the tub, Melanie said, "Set your knees there. Lean across the tub and press your hands flat on the far side. Kiss the tile."

After Kathryn left town, and years before she met Pasha, Melanie liked to give orders. And then, still before meeting Pasha, she'd been with a woman who taught her the joys of subservience. Now she was driven not so much by Pasha's will, but by her own resolve. Obedience was the gift she gave to Pasha.

The key was to obey before being told. That was Melanie's specialty.

Though Kathryn did need to be told, she obeyed without question. When her forehead met the tile at the far side of the tub, Melanie pulled her tight white dress up and over her smooth bottom.

What a sight.

Melanie glanced back at Pasha and smiled. "It's been a long time since I've seen an ass this fine."

Pasha's laughter swelled. "Is true!"

Melanie gave Kathryn's bum a few playful taps before hooking her index fingers around the white lace thong. "This is coming off." She pulled it down, all the way to Kathryn's knees.

One shoe and then the other fell from Kathryn's feet as Melanie offered the next instruction. "You're going to reach back slowly. With one hand and then the other, pull your cheeks apart. I want to get a good look at your asshole."

Kathryn inhaled sharply, but she didn't waste any time. She reached back with one hand. When she'd grabbed one cheek, she pressed her head against the shower wall and raised her elbow, sending the other hand toward her bum.

"How do you feel?" Melanie asked. "Comfy?"

"Mmm-hmm," Kathryn replied, although *comfy* hardly described her position. In a breathy whisper, she asked, "What should I do now?"

Without even looking in Pasha's direction, Melanie felt a smile growing across her Domme's lips.

"I told you to pull your cheeks apart," Melanie said in a slow, calm voice.

Kathryn gasped as her polished pink nails dug into her porcelain flesh. "What are you going to do to me?"

Melanie's heart fluttered as she watched that tight little asshole pucker. It looked so *real*. She loved that Kathryn's ass wasn't waxed, bleached, or perfect like porn star rumps. Faint wisps of blonde hair grew along the insides of her thighs, leading Melanie's gaze to the pink of her slit.

Kathryn's pussy was wet and welcoming, and it made Melanie a little sad to ignore its appeal.

But she had a Domme to please.

As Pasha looked on, Melanie said, "I'm going to fill you with water and rinse you right out."

Kathryn's breath hitched audibly as her fingernails dug into her flesh, but she didn't offer any resistance.

No sense wasting time. Melanie amassed saliva on her tongue, leaned forward, and spit in Kathryn's crack.

Kathryn issued a high-pitched squeal, but she didn't budge. When the dribble of spit kissed the crease of Kathryn's asshole, Melanie pressed the water bottle nozzle against it. If that's what Pasha wanted, that's what she would do.

"Is your head hurting, my dear?" Pasha asked.

"Mmm-hmm," poor Kathryn replied.

Melanie's heart slumped.

Was it fair for Melanie to impose Pasha's will on the sweet blonde who knew nothing of this life?

Ah, but it was Kathryn who'd asked for it. It was Kathryn who'd invited them back to this hotel room. Kathryn wanted this every bit as much as they did. If she was anything like Melanie, she loved to be surprised.

Pasha set both hands on Kathryn's white cheeks. "There you are, dear. I will hold them for you. You support yourself. It will relieve the pressure from your head, my poor sweet girl."

Melanie had always loved the way Pasha pronounced that word. It came out something like *squirrel.*

Girrel.

As Pasha held Kathryn's cheeks apart, Melanie pushed the nozzle just beyond her ass ring.

"Clamp down with your butt," Melanie instructed, though she could already feel Kathryn doing it.

When the bottle was in place, Melanie met Pasha's smile with one of her own. Kathryn's pretty little anus grasped the nozzle. Melanie used the strength of Kathryn's hold to open the top.

"I'm going to fill you now," Melanie warned her. "Don't you dare fight back. If you spray Pasha or me with ass-water, there'll be hell to pay. And you don't want to get shit all over your nice white dress, do you?"

Pasha's fingernails were too short to drive into Kathryn's skin, but she dug her fingers into that lovely flesh.

Kathryn whimpered, but she didn't move.

Wrapping both hands around the bottle, Melanie geared up for a constant squeeze. She applied pressure to the thin plastic bottle and sensed the stream of water soaring through the tip, straight into Kathryn's ass.

"It is not too hot?" Pasha asked as Melanie kept squeezing.

"Uh-uh."

Pasha spread her cheeks wider. "Too cold?"

"Uh-uh."

Almost imperceptibly, Kathryn's hips started moving. A little. Just a little.

Melanie couldn't believe it. The girl was actually fucking the water bottle as it slaked her ass!

That made Melanie grin. She knew just how Kathryn felt as warm water shot deep inside her body: Kathryn felt full. She felt pressure. But it was different from the pressure of needing to release her bowels. It was more like having to pee, but it was different from that too. Melanie knew no other sensation could compare. Pasha had put her through this humiliation more than once.

When she perceived resistance in Kathryn's body, Melanie stopped squeezing the bottle. She'd crushed it pretty badly anyway.

"What now?" Kathryn asked. Her voice sounded strained and desperate. "What do I do?"

"Hold it," Pasha said. "Hold still until my Melanie gives you instructions."

Melanie eased the water bottle from Kathryn's ass. Slowly. She didn't want to get squirted.

When it was out, she tossed it in the sink. Pasha released Kathryn's bum cheeks. They backed away in unison, standing side by side against the counter, like equals.

"Do not wait too long," Pasha said. "Or she will blow. And that will not be pretty."

Pasha was right, of course.

"Get on the toilet," Melanie said, helping Kathryn up from the tub.

With her dress pulled up her belly and her gorgeous tits popping out the top, Kathryn looked up at them. Her fawn eyes pleaded, and then she turned those pleas into words. "I have to go with you watching me?"

Pasha bowed to the princess on the throne. "That is correct, my dear Kathryn."

"Oh God," Kathryn moaned, dropping her elbows to her knees and holding her head in her hands. She was obviously clamping her ass muscles, trying to keep her body in check. Looking up at them with shame on her face, she covered her blonde bush with her hands and leaned forward. "I can't stop it!"

Melanie bit her lip and listened to the water streaming from Kathryn's ass.

How many times had Melanie been the one to get cleaned out? To be judged by other women's eyes while she released the contents of her colon?

It had been like living out a nightmare, the first time.

Then, after only a few repetitions, her embarrassment lessened until she'd unlearned the shame she was taught as a child: the shame of shit.

Kathryn tightened up her thighs. She probably figured if she created a tight enough seal around the bowl she could contain her stink. In truth, Melanie couldn't smell much beyond the apricot soap Pasha was now unwrapping.

"This is for the recycling bin," Pasha said, pointing to the bottle in the sink. "Empty the rest of the water and dispose of it, my dear."

Had Melanie neglected her duties?

She bowed her head and twisted the top off the bottle, emptying its mostly clear contents into the bathtub.

"There's no recycling bin in the room," Kathryn said in a whimper. "You'll have to take it to the ice room..." Kathryn pointed toward the hallway. She was staring at the floor. "At the pop machine, you know?"

Kicking herself for not disposing of her waste without being told, Melanie flipped the latch back on the hotel room door to prop it open. She raced down the hallway in her stocking feet.

The water bottle smelled like ass. Plastic had an incredible ability to retain scent.

She smiled sheepishly at an elderly couple's reaction as she zipped past them.

HOTEL BEDROOMS

Though she didn't leave the room for long, Melanie returned to find the big bed unmade.

Kathryn was on the fitted sheet with her face flat to the mattress and her clean ass in the air.

Pasha stood behind her, extending a soapy white cloth to Melanie.

"Finish the job," Pasha said, "and then lick it clean. Hurry up, my dear. You are taking far too long."

Melanie took the hot, soapy cloth in hand and circled it around Kathryn's ass. She slid the washcloth up Kathryn's crack from bottom to top, paying special attention to her prying little button.

When she removed it, that pretty little ass was red from the heat.

Holding her breath, Melanie turned the cloth around and looked at it.

Perfectly pristine.

White.

She let out a relieved sigh. If it had been dirty, even a little bit, she would have been compelled to start all over again.

"What should I do?" Kathryn asked as Melanie scuttled to the bathroom to toss the washcloth in the tub.

Pasha answered. "Wait a brief moment, my dear."

Melanie raced back to the bedside, magnetically drawn to that clean, blushing ass. "You don't have to do a thing, babe."

Setting both hands on those lovely warm cheeks, Melanie pushed them apart and geared herself up to take her first lick at Kathryn's crack.

The girl tasted like apricot soap. Not like ass at all.

Kathryn squealed as Melanie ran her tongue in circles around that pretty pink hole.

Eating ass was nothing like eating pussy. It was a hole without a clit, for starters. She could lick it up and down, she could lick it around and around, but she couldn't resist setting the tip of her tongue dead centre and poking inside.

That pretty little rosebud grabbed Melanie's tongue and held it like a vice. Clinging to her smooth cheeks, Melanie penetrated her hole in firm thrusts.

"Yes," Kathryn whimpered. "Yes, please... please, more!"

The tongue was a damn strong muscle, but Melanie's ached. Even so, she couldn't have stopped even if she wanted to.

This was her duty. This was for Pasha.

She pummelled Kathryn's asshole in and out, again and again, and when she needed a break from that she stuck her tongue in as far as she could get it and shook her head side to side. She pulled out and spit for lubrication, then licked, sucked, kissed Kathryn's pucker, finally sinking her tongue back inside.

Kathryn's juices dripped from her pussy to the bed in long sparkling strands of wetness.

Melanie just had to get her hands on that pussy.

With a pleading expression, Melanie turned to meet Pasha's gaze. "She's got the prettiest cunt, Pash. And it's sooo wet."

Pasha's lips remained sternly pursed, but her eyes glowed over a deep, dark expression of lust. "You may."

Setting her cheek against Kathryn's hot ass, Melanie reached between the girl's thighs. She loved the tickle of all that pubic hair. Melanie missed having a big bush like that, but once you start shaving it's hard to stop.

Sending her fingers through that expansive field, Melanie made a fist and tugged.

Kathryn whimpered like she was trying to keep quiet.

Maybe she thought that's what was expected of her.

"All this hair!" Melanie pulled on it, cupping Kathryn's mound. God, it was wet. She couldn't keep herself from rubbing the meat of her palm around Kathryn's hot cunt. "You've got the ripest damn pussy I've ever touched."

When Pasha cleared her throat, Melanie's breath hitched. She'd gone too far, said too much.

With a subtle nod for Pasha, Melanie occupied her mouth in the manner expected of her. Touching her tongue against Kathryn's asshole, she licked the puckered rim in neat circles. Her palm mashed Kathryn's pussy lips with the same motion.

With every pass, she avoided her friend's clit. She'd learned that from Pasha. It was the worst possible tease, feeling that divine pressure getting closer and closer to her hot spot, and then "No joy," as Pasha put it. Complete avoidance. A dip around it, passing just under her clit.

If only Pasha were doing this to Melanie right now, but she knew that wasn't going to happen.

"Are you licking our dear Kathryn's asshole?" Pasha asked.

Melanie didn't even realize she'd stopped until her Domme called attention to it.

She knew better than to make excuses. She simply said, "I'm sorry. I'll start again."

Kathryn's whole body went limp, and she whispered, "Oh God," like she was talking to a real live deity who was sitting right by her face... or maybe on it.

Up and down, side to side, round and round—Melanie licked Kathryn's asshole, but she couldn't seem to elicit more than the occasional squeak and moan. She worked that ass harder, licking like a dog, getting sloppy. Everything was wet now, saliva dripping down Melanie's wrist, mixing with Kathryn's pussy juice and frothing against her chin.

Finally, and most unexpectedly, Pasha stepped in.

"Our dear Kathryn seems not to be responding to your attentions." She bustled Melanie out of the way. "You are still learning, my dear Melanie. Pay attention. I will show you how to pleasure a woman."

Shocked, feeling like she was in a dream, Melanie suppressed the burn that was coursing through her chest.

Humiliation.

Pasha had accused Melanie of not being a good lover. In front of Kathryn.

Such profound humiliation...

The juice of Melanie's arousal ran slick against the gusset of her panties. Her clit throbbed so hard she could have sworn she was growing a stiff cock inside her slacks.

Kathryn was getting all the attention tonight. In a lot of ways, that was torture.

"My dear Kathryn, you have a beautiful asshole." Pasha's husky voice violated Melanie's sensibilities. "Roll onto your back so I can get a better view of your pussy."

At first, Kathryn did nothing. When she did move, it was to gaze over at Melanie, who was now perched against the mattress beside Pasha.

Melanie knew that look. Kathryn was seeking permission. It was sort of sweet, actually.

When Melanie nodded, Kathryn eased up on all fours, like a dog with its tail between its legs. She settled down cautiously in front of Pasha.

Melanie couldn't take her eyes off Kathryn's tits. Her nipples played hide-and-seek as she breathed, rising just above the top of her exposed bra before ducking back inside the cups. When Pasha urged her to raise her hips, her breasts swelled out and, God, did Melanie ever want to suck those little nipples.

"Not yet," Pasha instructed, always the mind-reader. "I want you to watch what I do to our dear Kathryn. You will learn, my girl."

My girrel.

Melanie nodded, even though Pasha's gaze was focused squarely on Kathryn's cunt. She pierced that begging slit—three fat fingers all in one go—and Kathryn bucked her hips even higher, squealing. Melanie could only imagine the intense sensation.

"You see what I do?" Pasha asked as she pulled her fingers from between Kathryn's swollen lips.

Melanie felt strangely like the host of a talk show watching her celebrity chef guest prepare a delicacy. She kept thinking, 'I know how to do this! I'm not stupid!' and then forcing humility upon herself.

Nobody was so clever they couldn't learn something new.

She watched as Pasha traced glistening juices all down Kathryn's ass crack. It was beautiful, the way Kathryn moaned and writhed on the bed while Pasha rubbed there.

"A clean asshole is a wonderful thing," Pasha said as she poked a fingertip inside, turning it like a corkscrew.

She didn't wait long before pressing a second one in, turning her hand, spreading her fingers to pry open that tight hole.

It really was an amazing thing to watch.

Kathryn's pussy lips fluttered noticeably as Pasha dug in deeper, forcing past resistance. She was so wet, so damn wet that her juices dripped down her thighs.

When Pasha's fingers were buried to the hilt inside Kathryn's tight hole, she turned her head and nodded. Melanie knew what that meant, and she hopped up on the bed, making Kathryn bounce and gasp.

That was just the beginning. When Melanie grabbed her friend's tits and pressed them together, Kathryn began to hum. The hum grew louder and rose in pitch when Melanie licked her nipples, weaving back and forth between those sensitive buds.

Kneeling at Kathryn's side, Melanie devoured those perky tits. She admired the concentration on Pasha's face as her Domme fucked the girl's ass. Kathryn's hum grew louder as Pasha pummelled her with two fingers.

Had anyone ever done this to Kathryn before?

Hardly likely. It inflated Melanie's sense of self to think that Kathryn was experiencing something new with them.

Rubbing Kathryn's nipples with her cheek, Melanie listened to the girl's raging heartbeat.

And then Pasha nodded ever so slightly to Kathryn's cunt, and Melanie didn't waste a second. She bent toward Kathryn's pussy, trying desperately to locate a clit somewhere within that pasture of hair. It tickled her nose, made her want to sneeze, but she held back, searching those sweet folds with her tongue.

Kathryn thrust against Melanie's face, bucking to meet Pasha's fingers. When she clawed at the sheets, Melanie could practically feel the assault on her asshole. She knew how good it felt to be washed out, to know you were all neat and clean down there, and then get rammed with fingers or a dildo or just about anything.

And getting her clit sucked all the while? What a lucky girl.

Finding the engorged nub of Kathryn's clit, Melanie sucked it into her mouth. Oh, so slippery-slick, like a little animal squirming under her tongue, seeking escape.

Kathryn was already so close that the burst of stimulation threw her right over the edge.

The girl in the tight white dress went wild, bucking hard, tossing Melanie off her like a bronco, screaming for mercy.

"Enough!"

But Pasha kept thrusting those big fingers inside her ass. Hard. Melanie envied Kathryn the experience, but she was pleased to realize she didn't feel jealous. She was satisfied to give pleasure, and experience it vicariously.

"Please," Kathryn hollered. "Please, you have to stop. Please, Pasha!"

With a wide grin, Pasha twisted her fingers out of Kathryn's poor little asshole and backed away until she was settled against the wall.

They were silent now, aside from Kathryn's panting and moaning and utterances of, "Oh God, that was good." Her shoulders rose and fell as she gasped through orgasmic breaths. Melanie just watched those wet holes flit and pucker and grasp.

Melanie waited for Pasha to say something like, "You see how I please a woman? You will learn, my girl."

My Girrel.

But it was Kathryn who spoke first.

Turning to meet Melanie's gaze, she asked, "What should I do now?"

Oubliette

M iranda couldn't put a lid on her temper. "What the hell do you call this?"

Saba sighed, but that only made Miranda angrier. She had every right to be upset, and it wasn't at all juvenile—even if Saba's expression implied that it was.

"Well?" Miranda asked. "You're not going to answer me? Yeah, that's the adult thing to do, Miss Passive-Aggressive."

Saba's posture relaxed, and she slumped on the hotel bed. They could never get through a vacation without some kind of blow-out argument. Why should this one be any different?

"Fine. If you're not talking to me, I'm not talking to you." Dressed only in her bra, panties, and a broomstick skirt, Miranda hunkered down on the harvest-gold sofa. Normally she couldn't forgive a hotel such dated décor, but she was willing to cut a converted castle some slack.

Miranda picked up the amenities binder from the coffee table. Usually that was the first thing she did when she checked in to a hotel, but Saba was in a giving mood when they'd arrived, and Miranda was happy to receive. She smiled just thinking about Saba's face between her thighs. When she glanced up, her girlfriend was staring at the ceiling, arms folded, lips pursed.

The castle housed one of those spas people raved about, but Miranda had never been one for fancy pedicures or mud baths. She was more interested in walking the scenic grounds and visiting the town's quaint artisanal shops. When she flipped the page and spotted a write-up for a ghost tour, she added that to her mental list. Miranda loved spooky stuff, and the idea of a haunted castle made her tingle.

"If you're waiting for an apology, you're not getting one." Saba kicked her feet off the bed and sat up in one quick motion. "I have every right to wear this ring. It belongs to me. It's *mine*."

"Not really," Miranda said, though that was the least of the reasons the ring made her mad. "When you break an engagement, you give back the jewels. It's common courtesy. When you're not engaged anymore, you don't wear the goddamn ring. That's a courtesy too, to your new girlfriend."

"You're overreacting," Saba said. "Now put your top on or we'll be late for dinner."

When Saba tossed Miranda her flowing peasant blouse, she caught it, but she didn't get dressed. "I'm not spending dinner fighting with you. Come on, we settle this now."

Saba was fully dressed and stunning in her fitted black gown—sleeveless, with what she called a "Breakfast at Tiffany's" collar laced with diamonds that looked real but weren't. She touched them as she spoke, like she was reading braille and translating. "I know why you're upset, but it's silly. I'm not in love with Raj. I never was. It was just family pressure. You know all this. Why am I telling you again?"

"Because you obviously don't get why it upsets me so much."

"It's just jewellery!"

"No it's not!" Miranda's mind was muddied with anger, but it was hard to explain her concerns. "If we were talking about a necklace or a bracelet, sure, but it's not. It's an engagement ring. You don't wear an engagement ring unless you're engaged, and you're not anymore, which must mean you're stuck in the past."

Saba rolled her eyes. "Seriously?"

"Are you still in love with him?" Miranda asked, even though that question always caused a meltdown.

Saba said no in every way possible. Loudly. Miranda almost told her to lower her damn voice, but there was something oddly satisfying about this argument. Every time Miranda put that question to her, Saba shouted about how much she didn't love Raj and how much she did love Miranda.

And, ultimately, she took off the ring.

By the time they'd calmed down, they were *way* late for dinner. They'd reserved a table overlooking the castle's sprawling grounds. The sun was just setting when they ordered, and once Miranda had handed off her menu to the server, she took time to stare fondly at her gorgeous girlfriend.

Saba gave her a weird look. "What?"

"I'm just so lucky." Miranda always felt gushy and gooey after a heated argument. "I've never been with anyone as beautiful as you, you know."

"Oh, you're being silly." Saba rearranged her cutlery.

"It's true. All the lesbians I knew at school were really sporty and butch. For a while, I wondered if femmes really existed."

"We're invisible." Saba smiled. "You look nice in a skirt, you know. Thanks for wearing one tonight."

"Only for you," Miranda said. "And only on vacation. I really don't like skirts. They feel weird and my legs get all tangled up. It's annoying."

Saba laughed, and that glittering sound infused their conversation throughout dinner. It wasn't until they were stuffing themselves with chocolate chili mousse that Miranda remembered about the ghost walk. "Oh shit! What time is it?"

With a shrug, Saba said, "I didn't wear my watch. It doesn't match my dress."

Miranda caught their server's eye and asked if they'd missed the tour.

"I'm afraid so," the woman replied. "They're probably halfway across the estate by now. If you'd like to catch them up, I can give you each a torch."

Despite the amorous glint in Saba's eye, Miranda itched for a ghost story before bed. She opted for the flashlights and dragged her girlfriend out the back door.

"I'm not wearing the right shoes for this," Saba objected while Miranda coasted down the gravel path.

"You'll be fine. They can't have gone too far. Wow, it's really dark out here."

"Nice to get out of the city," Saba said. "No light pollution."

Miranda was about to say, "I'm so glad we came here," when she heard the crack of a branch underfoot. Saba must have heard it too, because they stopped in their tracks at precisely the same moment. It happened again: footsteps in the wooded area beyond the path. Miranda grabbed Saba's arm and squeezed.

"I'm all goosebumpy," Saba whispered.

"Yeah, me too." Miranda clung even harder to Saba's arm. "Do you think it's an animal?"

"No, it sounds too big." Saba raised her voice to call out, "Hello! Is anybody there?"

Miranda had never listened so hard in her life.

"We're not too far from the castle," Saba said softly. "Why don't we head back?"

"No, I want to find out what it is." Miranda crouched down and aimed her flashlight into the bush. Even fully illuminated, the greenery looked dark. It was thick enough that she couldn't see what was making those noises. Probably just a skunk. She'd laugh if that's what it turned out to be. Laugh, and run.

And then another noise, a murmur. Like a baby. She strained to hear where it was coming from, or even what it was, but her heart thundered in her ears. It was hard to hear anything else.

Saba squeezed her shoulder, digging sharp nails into her flesh. "We have to go in there. Somebody's hurt."

"You think?" Miranda pried apart the branches she couldn't see past. She jumped when her flashlight caught a pair of eyes.

"What is it?" Saba asked. She must have spotted the eyes right after that, because she gasped. "Oh God!"

The whimpering grew louder, and Miranda steeled herself. Whatever this creature turned out to be, she could handle it.

"Hello?" she asked. "Who's there?"

The whimpering faded and there was a dragging sound in the woods. When Miranda illuminated the area, the eyes were much closer, right on the other side of the branches.

"Hello?" The voice sounded small and scared, so pained it broke Miranda's heart.

Saba must have been shaking, because her light wavered even as she stood still. "Can we help you?"

There was a pause, during which time Miranda worked up the courage to shine her light through the branches. When the harsh LED blueness illuminated the figure on the forest floor, Miranda felt strangely and suddenly calm.

"Help?" the young woman asked. Her face was gaunt and streaked with mud, like she'd been crawling through the woods for days, maybe longer. Her hair was an absolute mess, full of twigs and leaves and who knows what else.

"She needs our help," Saba said, taking a step forward before glancing down at her black leather pumps with faux-diamond wreathes.

"You're worried about your shoes?" Miranda asked. "At a time like this?"

"No." Saba hesitated before kicking them off. In her bare feet, she stepped into the branchy hedge.

Miranda held up a flashlight, astounded by her girlfriend's show of compassion.

"Come on, dear. I'll help you up. Just grab on to my shoulder. That's it."

The young woman shrieked when Saba hoisted her from the ground. The sound was blood-curdling, full of pain.

"It's okay," Saba said. "Let's get you on to the path, okay? One foot in front of the other."

"Foot," the girl whimpered. "Help. Foot."

When Saba drew the girl from the woods, Miranda gasped at the stranger's clothing—not because they were dirty, though they were, but because the fine velvet gown came straight from a bygone era. This woman must work at the castle. Front desk assistants and servers wore basic black, but historical interpreters were kitted up in fancy dress.

"You work here?" Miranda asked. "What happened? Are you okay?"

The girl clung to Saba with one hand, swatting the light beam like a kitten. She seemed incredibly agitated, especially when she started hopping on one foot. The other seemed badly cut, the wound encrusted with blood like it had been that way for weeks.

"Oh my God, Saba." Miranda pointed down with her flashlight. "She's really hurt. We need to find a doctor or something."

"No!" the girl cried.

"Let's get inside." Miranda nudged into the dirty girl's underarm so she and Saba each bore half the woman's weight. "It's going to be okay. Don't worry."

"What's your name?" Saba asked. "Do you live near here?"

"Oubliette," the girl said.

"Is that a name or a place?" When the girl didn't respond, Saba asked again, "Is that your name? Oubliette?"

The girl threw her face against Saba's long neck and wailed.

"She must be in terrible pain," Miranda said. "I hope there's a doctor nearby. Is there a hospital around here?"

"I miss civilization," Saba said.

Miranda knew the feeling. She couldn't wait to hand Oubliette off to someone who could help. The girl smelled absolutely rank, of sweat and urine and worse. How long had she been in those woods?

They entered the back door and carried Oubliette to reception. All the other guests must have taken the ghost walk or returned to their suites, because the lounge, games room, and hallways were deserted.

"Hello?" Saba called when they reached reception.

Oubliette screamed, her voice rife with pain.

Miranda rang the bell five times. "Hello? We need help. We need a doctor."

When nobody came to the desk, she lunged across it. Why wasn't anyone was back there? This place claimed to have all-night concierge service.

"No!" Oubliette cried, pressing her face into Saba's neck. "No, no, no."

"Where *is* everybody?" Miranda asked.

"Her foot looks bad." Saba looked pleadingly to Miranda. "Let's take her to the room. We can at least wash the wound."

"Oubliette?" Miranda asked. "Is that okay with you? Can we help you with your foot?"

Nodding eagerly, the girl chanted, "Help foot, help foot!"

"She must be in shock," Miranda whispered as they helped Oubliette up the stairs.

"Can you tell us what happened?" Saba asked.

The girl didn't respond right away, but when they entered the suite she started sobbing.

"Shh, it's okay." Miranda petted Oubliette's back, but she threw herself harder against Saba's front. "Wow, she really likes you."

"Guess so."

Miranda flitted away. What could she do to feel useful? Their clawfoot tub called to her, and when she filled it with warm water Oubliette eased away from Saba.

"It's for you." Miranda turned off the tap. "Do you need help getting in?"

"Here, I'll undo your zipper." Saba lifted the nest of hair from Oubliette's shoulders. "Oh. No zipper. Wow, these costumes they give you really are authentic, aren't they?"

Miranda and Saba worked at the girl's layers—gowns, skirts, and whalebone corset—while Oubliette glanced around like a mockingbird with too many shiny objects in her sights. When they released her from all that clothing, Oubliette seemed oblivious to her nudity. Miranda certainly wasn't. She and her girlfriend were standing in their hotel bathroom with a naked stranger. And a dirty one, at that.

"Here, we'll do this first." Saba grabbed a hand towel and dunked it in the bath. She nursed the girl's wound with more care and compassion than Miranda had ever seen. Just watching Saba's loving hands clean Oubliette's foot made her heart swell.

Oubliette wiggled and pulled away, but she didn't scream or shout. Maybe the wound looked worse than it actually was. Not that Miranda could concentrate while Oubliette's nipples hardened to dark pebbles. Those beautiful breasts made her horny as hell, and the bush on that girl made her feel wild. Miranda had never seen so much hair on a woman. Her legs, too! At first, Miranda thought they were just really dirty, but no—that was hair.

Once they'd helped Oubliette into the tub, Saba said, "We'll give you some privacy, unless you'd prefer that we stay."

"Stay!" Oubliette cried. "Stay, stay, stay! Help?"

The filthy girl looked at Miranda with the same pleading gaze her cat gave her when it wanted to be stroked.

"Of course we'll help," Saba said. "Whatever you need."

Miranda grabbed the luxury soap and tiny toiletries from the counter. "What would you like us to do?"

The girl didn't seem to understand. Maybe she couldn't hear very well? That would explain the trouble with communication.

"Want me to wash your hair?" Miranda asked, making her voice louder than before.

Oubliette's eyes gleamed. She leaned back in the tub, trailing her fingers from her cheeks, past her breasts, all the way down to her thighs. "Waaaaaaaaash," she said, drawing the word out so much Miranda luxuriated in its meaning.

Saba took hold of the soap while Oubliette dunked her hair under the water. When she came up, Miranda pulled twigs from that dark nest. She should have felt disgusted, so why was Oubliette turning her on so hard?

Getting her fingers good and soapy, Saba traced Oubliette's cheeks and forehead. The white suds turned instantly brown. Her clear bath had gone the same colour.

"I think you need a shower, Oubliette." Miranda poured the entire mini-bottle of shampoo into the girl's horrible hair and worked it in until her fingers hurt. The suds turned black. "How long have you been in those woods?"

Oubliette looked up at Miranda and smiled. She released a sleepy coo, letting her eyelids flutter closed. She only opened them when Saba reached behind her to pull the plug. Splashing dirty suds across the wall, Oubliette whipped around, soaking Miranda's white peasant top with black water.

"It's okay," Saba said. "Don't panic. It's time for a shower, okay? Here, take the soap."

Oubliette examined the filthy bar while Saba turned on the shower. When water cascaded from the fixture, the poor girl screeched. She scrambled, but the tub caught her shin. If Saba hadn't been there to catch her, that pretty face would have hit the slate floor. Hard.

Miranda chastised herself for feeling so aroused, but she couldn't help it. Saba struggled for breath as a stranger pressed bare breasts against her sopping-wet dress. Those naked tits looked so hot against Saba's that Miranda would have paid money to watch them kiss.

Dirty water rushed toward the drain as a clean flow splashed down on Oubliette's pert little bum. While Saba helped the girl wash all that gunk out of her hair, Miranda grabbed the soap from Oubliette and ran it over her belly and breasts.

"Miranda!" Saba said in a reprimanding whisper. "Have a little courtesy."

But Oubliette purred like a kitten, leaning half her weight against Saba while Miranda soaped her filthy flesh.

"Wash," the girl pleaded, pushing her breasts into Miranda's hands. "Wash, wash."

Miranda looked at Saba, trying not to say anything too snide.

"It's still customary to *ask* before touching someone," Saba said.

"You couldn't drop the self-righteous act for a minute, could you?"

Saba didn't look at her. "I'm not going to argue in front of guests."

"Wash!" Oubliette grabbed Miranda by the wrist and forced her hand between those dirty little thighs. The girl looked to Saba and put on a kittenish smile. "Touch?"

Saba's jaw swung open, as wide as her eyes.

"Go on." Miranda ran the soap through Oubliette's dark bush, getting it all soapy. Her top was so wet it clung to her skin. "You heard our guest. She wants you to touch her."

"Why don't I wash out all this shampoo, hmm?" Saba reached for Oubliette's hair, but wrinkled her nose at the dark mass. Much of the shampoo had already come out while the girl stood under the shower, but Saba worked the rest out while dirty water cascaded down her arms.

"You're getting soaked, huh?" Miranda teased. "Me too. You wouldn't believe how wet I am."

"Not the time," Saba said, but she couldn't hide her smile. "You're bad."

"Bad, bad, bad!" Oubliette opened her legs. "Wash." Her eyes darkened. "*Touch...*"

"Really?" Miranda wouldn't say no if the offer was real. She and Saba had always agreed it wasn't cheating if they did it together. "Are you serious, Oubliette?"

The girl parted her pussy lips, showing off the clean, glistening pink. "Touch. Please touch."

Miranda didn't want to look at Saba, because her reaction would determine whether this threesome was a go or a no.

"You're not in too much pain?" Saba asked. "Or shock? You're sure this is what you want?"

"Yes!" Oubliette cried, as if waiting for sex caused her physical pain. "Pleeeease!"

"Okay, then." Saba stripped off her dress and stepped into the tub wearing nothing but a smile. She gasped when Oubliette lunged at her, sweeping her into a full-bodied kiss.

A swift pang of jealousy burned through Miranda's chest, but the fire fizzled into a centralized ache as she watched two naked bodies writhing under the shower. They'd done a pretty good job of washing the dirt from Oubliette's skin, and it glowed a healthy pink against Saba's cinnamon flesh. They moaned into each other's mouths, pressing wet tits against wet tits, grasping each other's hips and asses.

"You guys look amazing." Miranda struggled for breath as she tore out of her soaked top and pushed down her skirt.

Stripping out of her bra and panties, she climbed into the clawfoot tub. Oubliette's backside was still a little dirty, so she grabbed the soap and got to work, scrubbing the girl's skin, rinsing it, rubbing her naked breasts up and down Oubliette's slick back.

Her hair looked like straw, so Miranda worked in the entire mini-bottle of conditioner. When Oubliette whimpered, she knew Saba must have found the girl's pussy. Miranda left the hair momentarily to glide her fingers down Oubliette's backside. She stopped when she got to the soft pucker of Oubliette's asshole. It pursed and winked, like it was nipping at her fingertip.

Oh, she couldn't resist. Miranda traced the perimeter in slow circles. When Oubliette really started thrusting at Saba's hand, she pressed inside.

Oubliette obviously loved the sensation, judging by her moans and stifled cries. Her ass ring clenched around Miranda's finger, hugging it tight, then relaxing... tightening, then relaxing.

"My God, what a pussy!" Saba moaned.

"Yeah?" Miranda touched her girlfriend's fingers through the thin wall that separated pussy from ass.

"She's so hot." They stroked in unison as Oubliette writhed in their arms. "She's so wet."

"She's so *close*." Miranda pressed her naked breasts against Oubliette's slick back, reaming the sweet girl's ass with not one but two fingers. "Rub her clit, Saba. Make her come."

Oubliette grunted as Miranda and Saba worked for her orgasm in a soapy mass of rubbing and thrusting. Conditioner ran from Oubliette's hair to make her backside slick. Miranda couldn't resist stroking her mound against the clean globe of Oubliette's ass, or reaching around to grab one of those magnificent soapy breasts.

"How's that?" Saba asked the girl. "You gonna come on my hand? Come all over my hand?"

"Good!" Oubliette threw both arms around Saba's shoulders and pulled her in for a kiss so scorching even Miranda could feel its heat.

Reaming the girl's ass, Miranda growled, "God, you're hot. I'm so glad we found you."

"Yes!" Oubliette bucked forward into Saba's hand, and then back into Miranda's. "Yes, yes, good!"

Arching under the shower, Oubliette tensed hard enough to trap Miranda's fingers in her ass. The girl's calves trembled and she gurgled without words as the shower needled them all. After a moment, she fell speechless into Saba's arms.

"Oh wow." Miranda couldn't shake the smile from her face, even as she withdrew from Oubliette's rear. "That was amazing, guys. I'll get us towels."

It felt amazing to make a woman come. When she and Saba worked as a team, there was nothing they couldn't accomplish.

They dried Oubliette head to foot, finding the odd patch of dirt where they hadn't cleaned thoroughly enough. After towelling each other off, Miranda and Saba wrapped Oubliette's foot in almost an entire roll of toilet paper, since they didn't have gauze.

Saba called the front desk, but there was still no answer. "How are you feeling, Oubliette? Are you sure you don't need a doctor?"

"No!" Oubliette screamed, falling to her knees and folding herself into a ball.

"Sorry." Miranda touched her softly. "We won't do anything you don't want."

When Oubliette looked up, her fearful gaze took on a lusty glint.

Holding her towel up with one hand, Miranda backed away, driven by a fear she couldn't name—and couldn't escape. Oubliette crawled across the Persian rug like a jungle cat. Situating herself between Miranda's thighs, she lifted the towel's edge.

"Oh my god." Miranda felt almost guilty that Oubliette hadn't chosen Saba to lick first, but she was hardly going to ask the girl to stop. "That feels so good."

Glancing between them, Oubliette smirked, playing sneaky, playing coy. She bowed between Miranda's thighs and went at it again. Her tongue was hot velvet, so practised and wet that Miranda couldn't help writhing against her face.

"That looks amazing," Saba whispered. "Oubliette, you're so beautiful, and Miranda, your clit's like a cherry."

Oubliette purred, and Miranda felt that sweet vibration against her clit. Still, she said, "Give Saba a taste."

Miranda opened Saba's towel and beckoned Oubliette inside. It worked. The girl crawled to Saba and landed between her legs, heading straight for the spot that would drive her wild.

"Holy fuck!" Saba grabbed Miranda's thigh, digging her nails in while Oubliette licked her clit. "Oh my god, you're amazing."

"She is, isn't she?" Miranda petted the girl's wet hair, then pinched her ear lobe. "You've got a talented tongue, Oubliette."

Saba fell back on the bed and moaned. "Holy hell, this is too much. Where did you learn how to do that?"

Oubliette giggled, and the prettiness of her laughter made Miranda so happy and horny that she needed some loving too. "Saba, baby, you'd better watch out because I'm gonna sit on your face."

"Go for it, babe."

Miranda dropped her towel. "Come on, let me eat your pussy, hon. You've had a rough time and you deserve as many orgasms as we can give you."

Oubliette crawled eagerly onto the bed, where they formed an easy triangle. The stranger didn't quit Saba's clit, not for a second. That eagerness aroused Miranda so much she nearly came the moment her girlfriend's tongue met her pussy.

"Wow, you're jumpy," Saba said, laughing.

Miranda groaned, throwing her face between Oubliette's thighs. Just one long lick to start things off, and not too hard, but it was enough to make the girl howl. Miranda pressed her pussy against Saba's face, rubbing all over her girlfriend's lips, chin, cheeks—anywhere.

"Mmm," Saba moaned.

Oubliette made the same sound, and Miranda joined in too. The girl's pussy tasted like flowers and buttercream. She'd never tasted anything so unbelievably delicious. Showing no mercy, she pressed her lips flush to the stranger's cunt, licking and lapping while the girl writhed on her face. Nobody could keep still. They were all so turned on by one another, and by the threesome itself, that they worked each other's pussies ruthlessly.

When Miranda felt a finger in her cunt, she got halfway to orgasm before talking herself down from it. She didn't want to come just yet. Saba stroked her insides, finding her G-spot, giving her that torture-feeling like she had to pee. She wanted this to go on forever.

"Bitch," Miranda moaned. "I'm gonna come so fucking fast if you keep doing that."

"Come!" Oubliette cried before going at Saba's pussy with noisy kittenlicks.

Miranda sucked Oubliette's clit like a fat nipple, making the girl moan. No, that wasn't good enough. She took

Oubliette's pussy lips fully into her mouth like she could swallow the girl's flesh. Shed nibbled, bit, chewed, anything to arouse a stronger reaction.

"Oh yeah, oh yeah, oh yeah," Saba chanted, like she always did when she was about to come.

Miranda wished she could see what Oubliette was doing to her girlfriend's pussy, but no way in hell she'd drag her mouth away from the stranger's sweet cunt. It tasted drastically different from Saba's. Too bad she couldn't taste both at once, or at least switch back and forth between them—sweet pussy, tangy pussy, flowery, then dark.

Saba stroked Miranda's G-spot in a finger-fucking frenzy. God Almighty, what a sensation! She didn't *need* to be filled in order to come, but it sure as hell didn't hurt. Her pulpy pussy clamped on her girlfriend's fingers, but it was far too slick and wet to keep those quick digits in place.

Oubliette panted like crazy on the other side of the bed, so hot Miranda could almost feel her breath baking Saba's skin. Oh, she was so close, so close. That warm tickle was taking over her belly, making her legs tremble and twitch. Nobody could scratch the itch quite like Saba.

"Oh my god, I'm almost there!" Miranda wrapped her lips around Oubliette's clit and sucked until it felt nearly as huge as a cock.

"Come." Saba stopped licking Miranda's clit and just tickled that spot... that spot... *that spot*. "Come now. Come all over my face, babe."

She couldn't have stopped if she wanted to.

"Oh god!" Miranda cried as a gush of fluid soaked Saba's face. Another spurt, then another. God, it felt good to let go like that. What a release.

Oubliette's kittenlicks got Saba off right after Miranda had come, and the girl from the woods followed swiftly behind. Their cries joined together like a duet Miranda longed to be part of, and she slammed her pussy against Saba's mouth until the duet became a trio.

Miranda had never come so hard in her life. She always got off on Saba's mouth, but to come twice in so short a time? That was rare indeed. It took all her energy just to right herself in bed, but she managed to settle on one side of Oubliette while Saba cuddled in on the other.

"In the morning we'll get your foot looked at." Saba sounded half-asleep. "Someone at the desk will know who you are. Someone will know..."

Miranda didn't even try to stay awake long enough to turn off the lights. She fell hard, and slept more soundly than she had in years. When she awoke, she had Saba cradled in her arms. For a moment, there was nothing strange about that.

Then the previous night came streaming back, and she asked, "Where's Oubliette?"

"Hmm?" Saba inched down to suck Miranda's tits, one and then the other, alternating between the two. Her girlfriend's sleepy affection made her mind melt, and she hoped the sweet suckling would never end. Never, never, never end...

Just when that warm mouth had lulled Miranda into a nearly comatose state, Saba sat straight up in bed, her eyes wide as dinner plates. "Oubliette?"

"Did you see her leave?"

"No. Did you?"

"Obviously not, or why would I ask?" Miranda glanced at the carpet beside the bed. Three towels. *Three*. "She was here. Now she's gone?"

Saba glanced at her night table, then touched the solid wood like she might feel something she couldn't see. "My ring was here, the ring from Raj."

Miranda didn't say anything. She was trying to remember if that was true, or if Saba had put it back in her luggage after their argument the night before.

"Did you take it? Was it you?" Saba's gaze struck Miranda not so much as threatening than as concerned. "Or was it her?"

"I don't know," Miranda stammered. Was Oubliette nothing more than a petty criminal?

"Where did she go?"

"I don't know."

"She's gone and so is my ring." Saba seemed agitated, and Miranda was too unnerved to calm her. "We'll go to the front desk. We'll report what happened."

"*Everything* that happened?" Miranda asked. She didn't want to share all the details.

A slow smirk bled across Saba's face, and it reminded Miranda of the pleasures they'd shared with the mystery girl. "We'll report a lost item. How's that?"

They dressed quickly and raced downstairs, where the friendly young man at check-in asked, "How can I help you this morning?"

"I lost a ring," Saba said. "It might have been stolen. I don't know. There was a girl in the woods. We tried to find someone, but nobody was here. We called from our room and no one answered and now my ring is gone."

The man's dark eyes opened so wide they were nearly all whites. "I think I might know what happened. Let me call in the expert."

"Security, I guess," Miranda said to Saba while he dialled.

"Frank, I have two guests who… well, they can tell you themselves." After he'd hung up, he said, "Our ghost expert will be down in a moment."

Saba laughed. For a moment Miranda thought the man must be joking, but it was clear from the concern in his eyes that he wasn't.

Frank was an older gentleman with wild white hair. "Follow me," he said. "Walk and talk."

Saba repeated roughly what she'd told the man at the desk, and by the time she'd finished her story, such as it was, they'd arrived at a dark stone staircase.

"Take a torch, please. Watch your step. Hold the handrail." Before starting down the stairs, he looked at them gravely. "You haven't attended my ghost walk, have you?"

"Not yet," Miranda said. "We were going to last night, but time got away from us."

Frank started down the stairs, and Saba followed, Miranda bringing in the rear. He told them a bit about the castle's history, which Miranda would have found interesting if she wasn't trying to piece together how it fit with Saba's stolen ring.

"As you can see," he said, "we are now in the castle's dungeon."

A chill ran down Miranda's spine, and when she reached for her girlfriend's hand she caught Saba trembling too. The castle's stone bowels made her flesh crawl.

"Maybe we've got our lines crossed," Saba said. "I was asking about a *ring*. My ring that was stolen. Or lost. I don't know yet."

Frank chuckled like he'd heard those words too many times to count. "No crossed lines, my dear. You've come to the right place."

Saba hated being called "my dear" but she didn't say anything, so she must have been desperate to find out what Frank had to say.

"Where are we?" Frank asked.

"In a dungeon?" Saba said, her voice tiny as a mouse.

"Precisely so. If you'd joined my ghost walk, you would know this dungeon housed baddies of all sorts. You might think it's a kind of hell on earth, but not so. Hell is in the corner over there, down that hole." Frank shone his flashlight into a space where the stone gave way to darkness.

"What is it?" Miranda asked. She wanted to rub her bare skin, warm it up a touch, but she was too scared to budge.

"That was a hole for people the royals wished to forget. And that hole was called..." Frank cocked his head, shooting them a knowing grin. "Well, you tell me."

Miranda's eyes filled with cold tears. She couldn't move a muscle, except those allowing her lips to pronounce the word, "Oubliette."

Frank applauded. "A history buff! Very good, my dear. Yes, indeed—that is the oubliette, the hole of forgotten people."

While Frank went on talking, Miranda shone her light on Saba's face. Her girlfriend was frozen like a statue, staring into oblivion.

"At the bottom of this oubliette, the uncommonly cruel Prince Rupert ordered spikes be laid. Anyone tossed into the oubliette would be injured severely, though not severely enough to die right away. Those poor souls suffered their final weeks hungry, thirsty, bleeding and infected, until they finally expired."

"Her foot," Saba whispered.

Miranda said, "I know."

"Did the prince ever throw a young girl in the oubliette?" Saba asked the ghost expert. "A young *woman*, I mean?"

"Yes, oh yes," Frank said, emphatically. "There is a most notable tale of the Princess Natassieka, who was hitched to Prince Rupert. Poor dear came to the castle, spoke not a word of English, and had to endure the Prince's cruelty in ways we shall never fully know. Her sole pleasure in life was the sensual company of her waiting maid. The women hid their affection for as long as they could, but a controlling man like Rupert was sure to find out sooner or later."

"Oh god..." Saba covered her mouth as tears streamed down her face.

"The prince ordered his doctors to perform all sorts of physical and psychological experiments dissuading the princess from her proclivity, but to no avail. Finally, the prince gave up on dear Natassieka and tossed her in the oubliette."

"What about the maid?" Miranda asked. "They loved each other. Did they at least die together?"

"That would make for a romantic tale, but no such luck," Frank said. "The maid was sent packing."

Saba bit her lip.

"You host a ghost tour," Miranda said. "Do people ever see Princess Natassieka around the grounds?"

"Yes, oh yes indeed!" Frank seemed strangely good-humoured for someone obsessed with hauntings. "Which brings us to your ring, young lady. I've heard many a tale from guests who've seen a full apparition of Princess Natassieka of the oubliette. Always women, mind. They say she leaves with something of value, something they've been holding on to perhaps too tightly, something they ought to forget."

"Wow." Miranda stared at Saba, but Saba was staring at the hole.

"Should I leave you ladies for a moment?" Frank asked. When neither answered, he said, "I'll be waiting at the top of the stairs should you need me."

"Thanks." Saba nodded without meeting the man's gaze.

When Frank was out of earshot, Miranda said, "Weird, right?"

"You can say that again." Saba threw her arms around Miranda, hugging her tightly. "I'm so sorry. Oubliette was right, or Natassieka, whatever her name was. She was right to take that ring. I should have given it back to Raj ages ago. Maybe I thought of him as my back-up plan or something."

Miranda stiffened. "Your back-up plan? What the hell do you need a back-up plan for?"

"I don't know." Saba took a step back, but held Miranda's hand. "Like, in case it didn't work out with us."

A burst of rage erupted in Miranda's chest. "You still love him?"

"No!" Saba laughed. "Honey, I never did. Honestly."

Miranda knew the truth. She felt it in her heart. Why was she constantly picking the same fight with her girlfriend? So what if Saba had been engaged to a guy? That was all in the past.

Glancing toward the staircase, Miranda spied Frank pretending not to watch them. The sight made her laugh. Despite the darkness, she was sure she caught a blush on Saba's cheeks when she leaned in for a kiss.

"I love you," Miranda said. "I don't want to fight about stupid stuff."

"I know, babe." Saba snuck her thumbs through Miranda's belt loops. "I love you too. I'm glad that ring is gone."

Saba's hot cheek warmed hers. This was all she wanted. Forever.

"I kind of wish we still had that ring. Then I'd have something to slide on your finger just now." Kneeling on the frigid dungeon floor, Miranda kissed her girlfriend's palm. "Saba, honey, I love you and I want to be with you from here to eternity. When we get home, can we start planning a wedding?"

Saba's smile could have guided ships in a storm. She yanked Miranda up from the floor and said, "You... are you... *seriously*?"

They hugged and jumped together, keeping their distance from the oubliette. In all their glee, the ghost expert's voice rang out clear as a bell. "I didn't hear a yes."

Saba laughed and cried and pressed her tearstained cheek to Miranda's. "The yes was implied!"

When they kissed for the first time as committed fiancées, Miranda could have sworn she felt a princess's wistful presence. For as long as she and Saba stayed together, she knew their love would be guided by a miraculous force. That was the essence of love: an everyday miracle.

Wedding Heat: Lickity Split

"**A** sundae bar at a wedding reception?" Kristen asked. "One of Pippa's brilliant ideas, I assume."

Shonette shook her head. "You're just jealous."

"Jealous?" Kristen cackled into her wine spritzer. "Nah, I won't fash myself on that wee nyaff." Her Scots lexicon only made an appearance when she was truly upset.

Of course, Shonette had no clue what Kristen was talking about, but she said, "Take a pill, Kris. It's a wedding reception, for Christ's sake."

"Och! And who holds a reception *before* the wedding? They're off their heads!"

"Would you lower your voice, please?" Shonette pulled Kristen away from the sundae bar, because other guests were staring. "Listen, you gotta calm yourself. First off, I don't understand half of what you're saying, and second, you *know* why the reception is today."

Everybody knew why. Maggie had explained it over and over: her parents insisted on a Sunday wedding, but the happy couple pushed for this luxury woodland resort weekend. If they held the reception Sunday after the ceremony, they worried guests would get behind the wheel after downing free booze. They couldn't stomach the idea of sending drunk drivers out on the highway.

So it was settled: they'd have a joint wedding reception/ rehearsal dinner on Saturday night, then high tea on Sunday after the ceremony. No alcohol. Safe highways. Win-win.

"I'm not jealous," Kristen mumbled. Her accent was fading, but her lies were clear as cellophane.

"Sure you are. You're jealous Maggie chose someone from her office as Maid of Honour. Who cares? Maggie made us bridesmaids. Isn't that good enough?"

With a growl, Kristen darted from the reception tent. Shonette chased her, catching her by the wrist, but she squirmed quickly away. As usual. Kristen always freaked out that someone might think they were lesbians.

"Where are you going, Kris?"

Anger flashed across Kristen's face. "I don't need some clarty lass hanging off me every hour of the day."

Clarty lass?

Before Shonette could process what was happening, Kristen took off, trudging down the path that led to their luxury accommodations.

"What a weirdo," said a voice at Shonette's back.

Shonette nearly jumped out of her skin, but it was only the bride's cousin Vanessa standing behind her. *Close* behind her. Too close for comfort.

"Sorry," Shonette said, though she wasn't sure why she was apologizing. "Kristen's a little stressed."

Vanessa cocked her head, eating a banana.

"I meant to ask before..." Vanessa hooked her thumb around her suspenders. "Are you Kristen's bitch, or what's the situation there? You're obviously fucking her."

"That's none of your..." Shonette's throat closed up. "I mean, what a question!"

Shonette took a big step away from the dyke in the fedora, but Vanessa only stepped closer. "Don't you straight-laced femmes know how obvious you are? Her pussy juice is all over your chin."

Shonette started wiping her face before realizing it was a metaphor. Still, she had every right to be taken aback. "That's no way to speak to a person. Watch your language!"

"What are you, ninety years old?" Vanessa slapped Shonette's ass hard enough to make her big butt quake. "You're young, Shon. Act your age."

"Oww!" Tears welled in Shonette's eyes. "Stop hitting me! And my name isn't Shon."

"Gee, I'm so sorry." Vanessa spanked her again.

"Why are you doing this?" Shonette shielded her ass from that vicious hand.

She expected the mean dyke to have some snarky answer. It surprised her when Vanessa asked, "What do you have against lesbians?"

Shonette wasn't sure what to say. Nobody had ever seen through her like this. "You spanked me. That wasn't nice."

Vanessa shrugged and looked away. "Just a little smack. I said I was sorry."

Rubbing her butt, Shonette glanced over Vanessa's shoulder. How had they gotten so far from the reception tent? They were almost in the woods.

Polishing off the last of her banana, Vanessa tossed the peel into the trees.

"Hey, don't litter!" Everything about this girl set Shonette's teeth on edge.

"It's organic. It'll decompose."

Shonette couldn't really argue with that logic. Still, the way Vanessa blocked her path to the tent sent a shiver down her spine.

"You never answered me," Vanessa said. "What do you have against lesbians? You *are* a dyke, aren't you?"

"No." Shonette could feel her face tightening. "Excuse me, please. I'd like to go back to the reception."

"I think you should check on your girlfriend. That bitch looked pissed."

"She's not my girlfriend," Shonette growled. "And she's not a bitch, she's just mad that Maggie didn't pick her as Maid of Honour."

"At least Maggie didn't pick *you* as Maid of Honour."

"Yeah, Kristen would have punched me in the face." Shonette surprised herself by laughing. "Hey, maybe that's why Maggie chose that girl from her office instead. She didn't want to create a rift between Kris and me."

Vanessa took off her hat and fanned her spiky hair. She must have been boiling in that formal trouser and vest combination. All the other women wore sundresses.

"So, are you and Maggie close?" Shonette wasn't sure why, but she didn't find the tough blonde so scary anymore. "Mags looked really happy to see you at the spa this morning."

"We were close when we were kids." The afternoon sun shone fiercely across the clearing. Vanessa shielded her eyes as she took in the scenery. "Not so much lately."

"That's too bad," Shonette said as they shifted toward the shade. "Most of my cousins live either in Guyana or in Germany. I'd love to see them more often."

"Oh, yeah?" Vanessa gave an exaggerated nod. "That's very interesting. Now tell what you've got against lesbians."

Christ, this girl would not let up! But, as much as Shonette didn't want to answer, she had to admit it was a fair question. "You're not going to tell Maggie?"

Vanessa rolled her eyes, which seemed like a strange response... but Vanessa was a strange girl...

"I don't have anything against lesbians," Shonette said. "I just don't want people thinking I *am* one. I guess that sometimes makes me go in the opposite direction, like being super-critical. Sorry, I'm stupid."

"Yeah, seriously." Vanessa flipped her hat back on her head, but arched it so the brim stuck almost straight up. "How long have you been licking your little friend's tang?"

"Do you have to be so crass?"

"Absolutely. So, how long?"

Shonette had never really thought about it, and the answer startled her. "Holy Crow... like, fourteen years?"

"Do you date other people?"

"We're not dating." Shonette leaned against a large maple, feeling the bark dig into her back. "We're not a couple."

"So, you see other people?"

"Yeah," Shonette snapped. "I mean, I could... if I wanted to."

"Do you want to?"

Shonette's chest felt itchy on the inside. "No."

"Does she?"

That was enough. "Why do you want to know? It's none of your business."

Vanessa's teeth gleamed as she grinned. "Isn't it?"

"No!" Shonette pushed herself away from the maple, but Vanessa blocked her path. For a slim chick, she sure made an impression. "Will you please get out of my way? I'd like some ice cream."

Vanessa didn't move. Not right away. So Shonette pushed past her and stomped toward the reception tent.

"I could go for some ice cream too, now that you mention it. Why don't we get a bowl for Kristen, and take it to your room? I assume you're sharing a room."

"What's that supposed to mean?" Shonette turned on a dime. "So what if we're sharing a room? Women share rooms all the time."

A snide smirk bled across Vanessa's lips. "Of course. You're right. You and Kristen mean nothing to each other. Now, let's get some ice cream."

They joined the line and picked up bowls. Shonette watched silently as Vanessa selected a bunch of barely ripe bananas. That girl thought she was God's Gift, didn't she? All she had to do was pick up a banana and every pretty femme would bend over and spread her legs. Well, Shonette wouldn't give in that easily.

"Grab that tray," Vanessa said. "We'll carry our bowls on it."

Shonette's thighs tingled as Vanessa hooked the bananas around her suspenders so they stuck out like three curved cocks. Her hands trembled as she served three flavours of ice cream into three bowls.

"What about toppings?" Shonette asked. There were chocolate, caramel, and strawberry glaze all in squeeze bottles. "Do you want any on your ice cream?"

"No." Vanessa grabbed one of each and fit the squeeze bottles onto their tray. After that, she made a beeline for the tent flaps.

Shonette followed fast, ignoring the waiter guy who was saying, "Excuse me, ma'am. The toppings need to stay with the sundae bar."

"Where's your room?" Vanessa asked as she marched across the clearing.

"Main building, second floor."

This was crazy! Shonette felt like a kid again, with the sun on her face, the wind in her hair, her cheery yellow dress whipping against her legs. She giggled as she kept pace with Vanessa.

"You're insane, you know." Shonette raced up the front steps and held open the main door.

With a wink, Vanessa said, "Baby, you ain't seen nothin' yet."

Shonette passed by the girl at the concierge desk. Her face must have been beet red as she and Vanessa ran up the central staircase.

"Which way?" Vanessa asked.

"Left." Shonette unzipped her purse and pulled out her room key. "Two-eleven."

Vanessa's dapper shoes skidded against the carpet. "Wha-hey! Unsupervised maid cart."

Shonette didn't stop until she'd arrived outside her door. "What are you waiting for?"

Shifting the ice cream to one side of the trays, Vanessa swept travel-sized lotions and potions onto the other. "Okay, we're good. Open the door."

Shonette's heart trembled. Kristen would be in there. No way she'd go along with this. At best, she'd be pissed that Shonette had brought Vanessa up. At worst... oh, she wasn't even sure what the worst-case scenario might be.

"Giddy up," Vanessa said. "Open the door. My arm's falling off."

Taking a deep breath, Shonette slid the key card into the slot. When the red light turned green, she swallowed hard. Grabbing the handle, she turned it just as the light flickered back to red.

"Kris?" Shonette called, holding the door open for Vanessa. "We brought you some ice cream."

"We?" Kristen rolled over on the bed. When she spotted Vanessa, she pulled the sheets over her naked breasts. "Oh, I... you... I wasn't expecting..."

Shonette's heart pounded, but Vanessa appeared unfazed. She carried the tray of ice cream and shampoo across the room, setting it on the mahogany desk. Shonette waited for her to say something clever, but she didn't say anything at all, just stared at Kristen like she could see right through that crisp white sheet.

"What's going on?" Kristen curled the sheet under her neck and tucked her legs right up against her naked body. "What are *you* doing here?"

"We brought ice cream," Shonette stammered.

Kristen's brow furrowed. "Fine, but why did you bring *her*?"

"Harsh!" Vanessa let out a bit of a cackle. "If I were anybody else, I might be offended."

"Maybe you should be." Kristen sat a little straighter in bed.

"You can kick and scream all you want, but either way you're gonna get smeared."

Kristen's eyes opened wide. "I don't know what that means."

Vanessa picked up a bowl of melting ice cream and scooped a little onto the spoon. "Shon, want to hold your girlfriend down while I spread this all over her body?"

"She's not my..." Kristen looked positively panicked as she glanced between Shonette and Vanessa. "What did she tell you? We're not... she's not..."

"I told her," Shonette said, catching Kristen's panic.

"Told her what?"

"I told her you're not my girlfriend!"

"You two are so full of shit." Vanessa cocked her head and looked at Shonette. "Or maybe you're not. Maybe it's one of those things where the people involved really are the last to know."

Kristen blinked, but said nothing.

"Know what?" Shonette asked.

That's when Kristen spoke up. "She thinks we're in love with each other."

Shonette's heart rumbled like thunder in her ears. Every sensible impulse told her to deny it, but...

"Hold her down," Vanessa said. "Will she struggle?"

"What kind of a question is that?" Kristen shrieked. "You're a nutter, plain and simple."

Shonette glanced at the dress she'd paid over two hundred dollars for. She slid down the zipper and slipped it off.

Kristen clutched the sheet. "What are you doing?"

"I don't want to get chocolate on it." Shonette hung her yellow sundress in the closet. "A chocolate stain never comes out."

"Ha!" Vanessa cackled.

"I must be drunk," Kristen said, falling back in bed. "Drunk, or dreaming."

"Tell yourself whatever it takes to get that sheet down." Vanessa mixed the chocolate ice cream into a sweet paste. "Come on, Krissy. Show us your tits."

"Go to hell!"

"Show us your tits."

"No!"

"Show us your tits."

Shonette caught the fever. "Yeah, show us your tits."

"Fine," Kristen said, like a brat. "You want to see my tits? Here!"

When Kristen flipped down the sheet, Shonette's pussy pounded. She'd seen that body countless times. It wasn't usually this exciting. Something about Vanessa standing there in the corner, staring at that body she'd never wanted to share... it was strangely exciting.

"Hold her down," Vanessa said. "Take off your panties and sit on her face."

Never in her life had Shonette been in a situation like this. Without thinking, she pushed down her underpants. Should she take off her bra too? No, not without Vanessa's instruction. She'd do what she was told. Nothing more, nothing less.

It was like a dream, when Shonette straddled Kristen's head, hovering high above her face. The night before, they'd played in this very bed. They'd slept in it. Together. Even so, it went without saying that when they booked the room, they insisted on two beds.

"Straddle her. Good." Vanessa's smirk was like chocolate—chocolate spiked with chili peppers. "Put your knees on her shoulders. Very good, Shon."

"Her name is Shon*ette*," Kristen said.

"I'll call her what I like." Vanessa teased her ice cream with a spoon. "What do *you* care? She's not your girlfriend."

"So what? She's still a bloody *good* friend. I still bloody *care* about her."

Shonette warmed when she heard those words. Kristen had never said anything so blatantly complimentary in all the time they'd been together. Well, not *together*, but... whatever this was.

"That's a start." Vanessa handed Shonette a squeeze bottle, then climbed between Kristen's legs. "Now, time for ice cream."

"Mmm, ice cream." Shonette's mouth watered as Vanessa blotted Kristen's belly with the sticky stuff.

"No! It's cold." Kristen arched until her abs quivered.

"You betcha," Vanessa laughed as she spread a line down Kristen's abdomen.

Kristen shuddered. Her legs trembled, but with her feet pinned under some very tight sheets, she wasn't going anywhere. Those pale tits swelled while their pretty pink nipples stiffened to buds.

"Chilly much?" Vanessa traced more ice cream around Kristen's belly button.

"I can feel it in my spine!"

"That's a shame." The ice cream melted against Kristen's light skin, but Vanessa only piled on more, all the way up to her breasts. "How do you think it'll feel when I top your tits with this stuff?"

"No!" Kristen wrestled so hard she almost knocked Shonette off her shoulders. "God, it hurts. It's too cold."

"Sorry, Kris," Vanessa teased. "Looks like I'm out of chocolate. Maybe Shon and I will just lick up what's here and come back later with the strawberry."

"Sooo cold..."

Shonette's pussy juice drizzled down her trembling thighs. Her clit throbbed like crazy, but she couldn't stroke off on Kristen's tongue until Vanessa gave the go-ahead.

"Should I top her off with chocolate syrup?" Shonette asked hopefully.

Vanessa hadn't stopped grinning since this all started. "Good idea, just don't get any on her boobs. I'm saving those for later."

"Ohhh!" Kristen kicked her feet against the mattress like a toddler throwing a tantrum. "My stomach's got frostbite. Just lick it up, if that's the plan!"

"Calm down, Krissy." Vanessa set down the empty ice cream bowl and grabbed Kristen's thighs. "That's a good girl."

"She *is* a good girl." Shonette squeezed chocolate sauce all over Kristen's belly. "Actually, I'd call her a goody-goody. She hates a mess. She hates getting dirty like this." Shonette squeezed out more chocolate, getting in on the fun.

Vanessa's grin stretched wider. "I had a feeling."

"We've never done anything like this before." Shonette set the squeeze bottle on the bedside table, and then leaned forward. "Do we eat now?"

"You'd bloody better!" Kristen shrieked.

"Don't get your panties in a bunch." Vanessa bent down, then glanced at her crisp white shirt. "Ooh, don't want to get this covered in chocolate."

Unbuttoning her shirt, Vanessa slipped it off without removing her black suspenders. She had tattoos up and down both arms. All that ink made Shonette's pussy pulse. Instead of a bra, Vanessa wore a tight white undershirt. It was threadbare enough that her pointed pink nipples showed right through the fabric.

"What are you two staring at?" Vanessa asked, still grinning. "You're like a pair of sex kittens ready to pounce."

Could Kristen see Vanessa from that position? Shonette hovered high enough over her head that it was possible. But that wasn't the important part. What did it say about them that they were both all gushy and greedy for a hard-core dyke?

"I thought you were dying of frostbite." Vanessa traced her fingers between Kristen's pussy lips. "You don't seem cold here."

As Vanessa stroked Kristen's clit, a twinge of jealousy hit Shonette in the heart. Sure, she could get the girl off, but it always took a good half-hour of dedicated licking. All Vanessa had to do was touch the girl's clit and, Christ, Kristen was biting Shonette's thigh!

"Let's get licking," Vanessa said, and bent to lap ice cream from Kristen's soft belly.

"Oh, god!" Kristen's body fluttered while Vanessa kitten-licked her middle. Shonette's jealousy ramped up a notch, but she wasn't sure where to focus it.

Vanessa glanced at Shonette. Ice cream and chocolate syrup were smudged across her nose and her cheeks. "Well? What are you waiting for?"

"Nothing. Sorry." Shonette held her long hair back and bowed to Kristen's skin. She'd never been a huge fan of ice cream, but coming off that sweet, salty flesh, it danced deliciously on her tongue. "Mmm... that's good."

Shonette and Vanessa came at Kristen from opposite directions, both hovering over her luscious belly. The first time their shoulders touched, Shonette jerked away. Vanessa must have noticed, because she kept nudging Shonette after that—creeping closer, nudging her shoulder, creeping closer, nudging. It was a tease, a very conscious tease. Vanessa could obviously tell the touch-touch-touch made her uncomfortable. Shonette tried not to feel it, and concentrated on lapping melty ice cream off Kristen's body.

"It's not cold enough," Vanessa said, and jumped off the bed. She picked up the bowl of strawberry ice cream. "Had enough chocolate, Shon? Get out of the way so I can put this stuff on your girlfriend's tits."

Kristen whimpered, but she didn't say no. Her belly was sticky with chocolate sauce when Vanessa took up the spot between her legs and slathered Kristen's breasts with pink ice cream.

"Don't forget the strawberry sauce," Shonette said. "Want me to get it?"

"No," Vanessa replied. "I want you to sit your snatch down on your girlfriend's face. Go on, Krissy. Eat Shonna's sweet pussy for me."

"God!" Kristen cried. "That stuff's so cold…"

By some miracle of nature, the solid scoops of ice cream stayed piled on Kristen's breasts even when Vanessa jumped off the bed. They didn't even budge when Shonette lowered herself on Kristen's face.

"Is this okay?" Shonette asked when she felt the warm kiss of Kristen's lips against her clit. "I'm not crushing you, am I?"

"Mmm-mmm." Kristen shook her head, but only slightly.

Vanessa watched from beside the desk. "Is she licking you?"

"Who, me?" Shonette asked.

Vanessa rolled her eyes.

"Sorry… no, not yet. You want her to?"

"You two! Fucking Tweedle-Dee and Tweedle-Dum!" Vanessa picked up the ice cream tray and tossed the whole thing on the bed. "How did you cope before I came along? Yes, I want her to lick your fucking pussy. And because she couldn't figure that out on her own, I'm leaving that ice cream on her tits. Shon, make sure those scoops stay put."

"Nooo!" Kristen cried into Shonette's pussy. The word resonated through her body, making her shudder. "Sooo cold!"

Shonette could feel the tension in Kristen's body, but for some reason she trusted Vanessa to get them both off. The melting ice cream sat like pink meringues on top of Kristen's beautiful breasts. Leaning forward, Shonette cupped them so they wouldn't jiggle too much.

"Is she *still* not licking you?" Vanessa growled. "My *fucking* lord, what is your problem, Krissy? Do as you're told, and do it now."

Shonette bit her lip, waiting for Kristen's velvet tongue to meet her clit.

"Who do you think you are?" Kristen pushed her voice out from where it was buried in pussy. Shonette knew that pissed off tone all too well.

"I'm the dyke who's going to save your fucking relationship. That's who I am."

"We're not in a relationship!" Kristen howled.

Usually, Shonette would have taken that as a simple statement of fact, but today the sentiment made her heart ache.

"Like hell you're not." Vanessa spread Kristen's legs and piled vanilla ice cream on her splayed pussy. "You're in denial, that's what you fucking are."

Kristen howled as the cold set in. Without thinking, Shonette bent forward and pinned her hips to the mattress. "Stay put and lick my fucking clit."

"Shonette!" Kristen cried, sounding very surprised. They never spoke that way to each other. They *never* talked about the things they did in bed. They just fumbled in the dark, found what they wanted, and took it. Never in broad daylight. Never meeting eye to eye.

"Tell her again," Vanessa said, heaping more vanilla on Kristen's crotch. "Be firm. Make her obey."

"Okay." Shonette glanced between her legs, but all she could focus on were Kristen's strawberry tits. "Kris, I'm not kidding. I want you to eat my pussy, just like Vanessa said."

"The ice cream's cold!" Kristen's lips quivered against Shonette's pussy. "So fucking cold!"

Shonette didn't want Kristen to be uncomfortable. She told Vanessa, "You're torturing her!"

"What was your first clue?" Vanessa squirted caramel sauce over Kristen's vanilla mound. "Ooh, that's looking better. Are you a fan of caramel?"

"Yeah, big time." Shonette's mouth flooded just looking at that sweet pile of cream and sugar.

"What about your girl? Does she like strawberry?"

"Yes!" Kristen shouted. Her mouth was starting to move now, her warm tongue gently massaging Shonette's pussy.

Vanessa aimed the strawberry squeeze bottle at Kristen's tits, but when she sprayed the gooey red stuff, it shot up Shonette's belly. There was strawberry sauce everywhere, all over Kristen and Shonette, glistening in the sunlight that poured in through the window.

"My tits!" Kristen cried. "My clit—it hurts so bad! Get it off!"

"I will, I will." Vanessa seemed pretty relaxed about the whole thing. "But no ice cream sundae is complete without a banana."

"What?" Kristen whimpered.

Vanessa broke one of the green bananas off the bunch that was still hanging from her suspenders.

"You're not..." Shonette sat harder on Kristen face to keep her from seeing. "You can't just stick a banana up my girl's snatch!"

Vanessa grinned. "So now she's *your girl*, is she?"

"Shut up! That's not the point."

Kristen's tongue slowly lapped Shonette's clit, making it hard to concentrate on anything else.

"What *is* the point?" Vanessa asked.

"It's not clean!"

Vanessa tapped Kristen's thigh with the green banana. "What a prude."

Kristen obviously wasn't opposed to the idea of getting fucked by a banana. She licked Shonette's clit more enthusiastically than ever. Shonette rocked on her face while Vanessa pawed through stolen maid cart items.

"What are you doing?" Shonette asked.

A shower cap! Vanessa wrapped the thin plastic over the banana and held it up in the air. "How's that for safer sex?"

Shonette gasped. "You're crazy."

"So I've been told." Vanessa held her banana like a weapon.

"I don't know if Kristen's going to like this," Shonette said as she rode that pretty pink tongue.

But Kristen knew. She hollered, "Fuck me!" and the words filled Shonette's pussy. "Fuck me now!"

Vanessa raised an eyebrow. "Your girlfriend knows what she wants."

Shonette didn't have a snappy comeback. Her brain was too addled by lust. While she rocked on Kristen's face, Kristen dug her fingernails into Shonette's ass. They both groaned as Vanessa planted that big banana in Kristen's cunt.

"This ice cream's melting fast," Vanessa said. In a surprise move, she grabbed Shonette's head and pushed it down to that pile of vanilla ice cream. "There we go, Shon. Show her how *you* want to be licked."

Shonette wasn't going to argue with her mouth full of caramel sauce. Besides, she kind of liked the idea. She swallowed ice cream that was just this side of frozen, then let her tongue explore Kristen's folds. God, they felt cool against her tongue. Kristen's pussy was usually so hot.

"She's got a pretty little pussy, your girlfriend." Vanessa grabbed the banana and shifted it gently inside Kristen's cunt. Kristen shrieked, and then moaned, and Vanessa wasn't even being rough.

On the rare occasions Kristen spoke up in bed, it was to say that Shonette was being too gentle, that she ought to go harder. Shonette always worried she'd hurt Kristen, but it was out of her hands today. Vanessa had a banana, and she knew how to use it.

"Come on, Shon. Get licking. You too, Krissy." Vanessa jerked the banana gently, like she was making an effort not to slam it in Shonette's face. "This girl's got it bad. You treat her right. Lick her good."

Shonette looked up from Kristen's vanilla-flavoured pussy. "What about you?"

"What about me?"

Kristen's strawberry boobs pressed against Shonette's belly, sticky and cold. "You've still got your clothes on."

Vanessa fucked Kristen a little harder. "Yup."

"You're not going to join in?"

"I'm already fucking your girlfriend with a goddamn banana. What the hell else do you want from me?"

Maybe it was too much to ask, but Shonette arched up. Her pussy still pressed against Kristen's mouth, but her chest surged in the air. "Here. Suck my tits."

Shonette's bra was a mess—covered in ice cream and syrups—but all Vanessa had to do was pull down the cups. Would she do it? All she seemed to care about right now was plunging that big banana into Kristen's pussy.

Not that Shonette could really complain. The harder Vanessa fucked Kristen, the faster Kristen licked Shonette's clit.

"Please?" Setting most of her weight on Kristen's face, Shonette tugged her bra down, exposing her big breasts. "Please suck them? It'll make me come. I love it so much."

"What about your girlfriend? You're supposed to be licking her clit, slacker."

Vanessa was really ramming Kristen with that banana, pounding her pussy, thrusting hard and fast. If Shonette got her face in there, she'd likely get punched.

"What if I do this instead?" Shonette found Kristen's sticky clit with her fingers. "I'm pretty good with my hands."

Kristen screamed into Shonette's ripe pussy.

"Oh, Shon, your girlfriend likes that!"

Smiling, Shonette stroked her girl's clit in tight circles. Kristen pressed her face right up close to Shonette's pussy. No more casual licks, nothing prim or pretty. No way. Kristen pushed her whole mouth against Shonette's cunt and sucked her swollen pussy lips. Sucked them *hard*. Not just her clit. *Everything*.

"You're doing something right," Vanessa taunted. "Shon's going wild!"

Shonette's big tits waved as she rode her girl's face. They'd never fucked like this. Never.

"Come on." Shonette met Vanessa's wolfish gaze. They worked together on Kristen's tender pussy, but Shonette knew what she wanted. "You think you're a tough dyke? Prove it. Suck my fucking tits. Suck 'em 'til I come."

The banana slowed in Kristen's pussy as Vanessa stared at Shonette's breasts. She looked half hypnotized.

Kristen released her suction hold on Shonette's pussy long enough to scream, "Fuck me, you bloody bitch! Fuck me hard!"

"You heard the lady." Shonette scoured Kristen's clit, riding her face. "Kris wants a fuck, I want a suck, so get on it. What are you here for if you're not gonna get us off?"

That was a good question, actually: why the hell *was* Vanessa in their bedroom when Maggie's pre-reception party was well under way?

If Shonette's brain hadn't been so fried by the prospect of orgasm, she might have dwelled more on that. Instead, she grabbed Vanessa by the undershirt and pulled the bitch against her sticky chest.

"Are you gonna suck my tits?" Shonette ran her fingers through Vanessa's spiky hair. "Or do we have a problem?"

"No problem," Vanessa said, sounding almost scared.

"You want my tits?"

"I want them," Vanessa bleated. "I want them. I want your tits."

"Yes!" Kirsten cried, bucking for more banana. "Yes, fuck me!"

Vanessa wrapped her lips around Shonette's nipple, and the warm suction put her right over the edge.

"Fuck!" Shonette played with Kristen's swollen clit while Vanessa suckled her. The girl was bent at such an awkward angle that Shonette relieved her of banana duty. "That's better."

"God, these tits!" Vanessa curled around Shonette's front, pressing her side into the sticky mess on Kristen's belly. "So fucking good..."

Kristen never got this excited when Shonette fucked her, but that was about to change. Shonette slammed the banana into Kristen's snatch until her body trembled with a full-body orgasm. Shonette felt Kristen's climax spread like radiant heat. It wasn't just in her belly, and it wasn't just in her clit. Her breasts swelled. Her thighs twitched. She'd never known Kristen to experience an orgasm like this.

Then again, they'd never had a threesome before.

"Feels so good," she told Vanessa. "Suck harder! Harder!"

Both Vanessa and Kristen sucked her flesh into their hot mouths, building so much force that she lost it completely.

"God, that's *amazing*!" Shonette started slapping Vanessa's face with her tits while she rammed Kristen hard. "It's so fucking good!"

"Don't tell *me*," Vanessa said. "Tell *her*."

Kristen's hot mouth put so much pressure on Shonette's clit that she felt like a big pool of melted ice cream. Could she really do it? In the heat of the moment? Could she tell Kristen how she really felt?

Shonette could feel Kristen's muscles clamping down on the banana, milking it. The air smelled sweet. Everything was sticky with sugar. That's when Kristen pulled away from Shonette's pussy and cried, "Fuck, that's good! I love you, lass!"

"You do?" Shonette's heart fluttered. There was so much to say, but she started with, "I love you too. I love you forever."

Now wasn't the time for lengthy declarations. Her brain was gone. No more words, just a panting, exultant, throbbing, wet orgasm. They exploded, all three of them. Even Vanessa yelped and hollered, like she was getting off on sucking Shonette's tits.

Shonette writhed and twisted on the bed. Ungluing herself from Kristen's sticky skin, she toppled to the side. Vanessa went with her, like one of those animal babies on nature shows, adamant about feeding even when their mamas have had enough. Shonette playfully pushed her away, and she laughed.

"Look how messy we are." Kristen wagged her finger at Vanessa. "This one's a bad influence."

"I'm surprised they haven't sent a search party for us," Shonette said. "The rehearsal dinner, or reception, or whatever they're calling it—it must be well underway by now. We'd better get cleaned up."

Vanessa shook her head. "You two are *so* vanilla."

"Probably, mostly," Kristen agreed. "But when you're mostly vanilla, it only takes a touch of chocolate to really shake things up."

"Or strawberry," Shonette said. She realized she was making puppy dog eyes at Kristen. Were they really as obvious as Vanessa said they were?

Prying herself off the chocolate-covered sheets, Kristen said, "If you'll excuse me, I think I'll be the first to take a shower."

Vanessa looked like she was going to shit herself. "*What? You two don't shower together?*"

"No." Kristen stood from the bed, and melted ice cream ran in streams down her legs. "You can't get clean when you're trying to get dirty."

Shonette leaned off the bed to lick strawberry sauce from Kristen's breast. She could sense Vanessa watching, and she liked it. She never thought she'd be one of those girls who got off on being watched, but maybe she wasn't quite as vanilla as everybody thought.

"Enough," Kristen said with a laugh. She knocked Shonette's head away and set off for the shower.

When Kristen had closed the bathroom door and turned on the water, Shonette shook her head. "You know, when she stormed off earlier, I thought she'd never go to bed with me again. She seemed really mad that I wasn't agreeing with her. I can't believe how wrong I was."

"I can." Vanessa squirted a good stream of strawberry sauce into her own mouth. "Jesus, I'm starving. I wonder what they're serving for dinner."

Shonette half wanted to ask what Vanessa meant by "I can," but instead she said, "I really owe you one. Kris and I would never have admitted what we meant to each other if you hadn't forced the issue."

"Sure you would." Vanessa sprayed Shonette with strawberry sauce, and she shrieked. "It just would have taken you another fourteen years."

Stealing strawberry sauce from her breast, Shonette sucked her finger. "Probably."

"So, no more shitting all over dykes, okay? Unless they really want you to."

"Eww!" Shonette laughed. "I'm not into that sort of thing."

"Oh, right. I forgot—you're vanilla."

"Everything but my skin. That's more caramel, I'd say."

Shonette waited for Vanessa's snappy comeback, but what she got instead surprised her.

"Hey, I owe you an apology." Vanessa pinched her thigh. "I came on way too strong. I know it's not an excuse, but I'm trying really hard to get over someone."

"Another girl?"

Stupid question, but Vanessa just nodded. "Yeah. I've been in love with her forever, but she loves someone else, so..."

"Hey, her loss. Right?"

"No, it's my loss. My big fat fucking loss." Vanessa shook her head, looking like she was actually in pain. "I don't deserve her anyway."

Shonette would never have imagined feeling sympathy for Vanessa, but she did. She set her sticky arm gently around Vanessa's shoulder. "I'm sorry."

"You don't know how lucky you are, having someone like Krissy." Vanessa smiled forlornly. "I'm proud of you two crazy kids."

"We've never exactly been adventurous in bed, but I think that's because we were both so scared."

"Scared of what?"

"Scared that if we called a spade a spade, everything would all fall apart. I thought she didn't want a relationship. I thought if I asked her to be my girlfriend, she'd call me a dyke and run away."

"Hey, live and learn." Vanessa gave Shonette a playful punch on the shoulder.

Shonette laughed. "You're such a guy."

"Hey, when Krissy comes out of the shower you should ask her to marry you."

"Yeah right." Shonette grabbed a pillow and threw it at her. "Hey, pillow fight! Isn't that what lesbians are supposed to do in hotel rooms?"

"Damn it, and I left my pink nighty at home!" Vanessa whacked Shonette with the pillow, getting sticky sauces all over the case. "Oh well. You're going down, lady."

Shonette grabbed another pillow and whacked Vanessa, giggling so hard her sides started to ache.

"Fuck, the maid's gonna murder us. Look at this bed!"

They both slipped off the mattress and looked at the filthy, rumpled sheets. In the next room, the water squealed off. Shonette listened intently as Kristen opened the squeaky glass door.

"Next time that girl takes a shower, you sure as hell better slip in there with her." Vanessa tossed her pillow to the head of the bed. "Trust me—I know things."

"I *do* trust you. I'm not sure why. Oh, hey, are you coming to Maggie's bachelorette party tonight?"

Vanessa's expression went blank, but she asked, "Where is it?"

"In her cabin." A wicked streak ran through Shonette as she thought about the supremely un-vanilla party they'd planned for Maggie. "We're all leaving the reception at eleven, and you would not believe what's going to happen. We've ordered these.... *people*... who come in and..."

The bathroom door opened and Kristen emerged in a white cloud of steam. Even in a terrycloth robe, she looked like an angel.

"You don't know how lucky you are," Vanessa said.

But that wasn't true.

Waxing is for Pussies

"Hey there, Soo Jin." I shot the cool receptionist a dapper smile. "How's tricks?"

"Pretty kick-ass, except my feet are on fire." Soo Jin's pink lips puckered as she raised an eyebrow. "Maybe I'll ask Billie for one of her *magic* pedicures."

One year ago I'd have been all over that, but Billie was my number one girl now. No slim Korean salon receptionist could tempt me away. Anyway, Soo Jin was just teasing about the time Billie ate me out in one of their big-ass pedicure chairs. No secret was safe in this place.

Soo Jin eyed the small tray of sushi in my hand. "I see you brought Billie some raw fish to snack on."

"Yeah." I couldn't believe the zingers this girl was getting off me. "I'm surprising her. Is she with a client?"

I didn't actually wait for an answer before clomping through the salon to find my girlfriend. I knew where her station was. Plus, my impromptu visit wouldn't be complete without pissing off her boss, Sandra. Queen Sandra of the Salon gave me the dirtiest looks every time she saw me. What didn't she like? The brush cut? The ink? The ripped cargo shorts? I had so many fine dykish qualities to choose from.

"Claire, wait!" Soo Jin traipsed after me in knee-high stiletto boots.

No wonder her damn feet hurt. *Wear sensible shoes, woman!* Not that I objected to the look. In fact, a nice pair of heels was usually the first thing I noticed about a girl. Billie's hot pink patent leather ballet slippers were the first things I'd noticed about her.

"Billie's with a client," Soo Jin said, click-clacking along the laminate floor. "Leave lunch with me. I'll give it to her when she's done."

Desperation rang out in Soo Jin's voice, but I couldn't understand why. I visited Billie all the time. When Queen Sandra was away, I spent entire days watching her work. Nobody cared. Even Billie's mani-pedi clients didn't care.

"Billie?" I did a double take, but Billie wasn't anywhere near the pedi chairs and mani tables. "I brought you lunch, babe."

I stood brain-dead, watching the one aesthetician whose name I could never remember apply shimmering peach polish to a MILF's fingernails.

Where was my girlfriend?

When Soo Jin caught up with me, I turned to her and said, "Billie's not here."

Soo Jin's gaze darted around the room, finally settling on the curtained area in the back corner where a woman named Luz did waxing. It was the only private space in the salon, apart from the washrooms and Sandra's office.

The guilty look on Soo Jin's face told me my girl must be holding a "private" gathering of her own. I stormed to the waxing room. Two dainty feet in hot pink patent leather ballet slippers stood alongside matronly flats.

Whispers behind the curtain. *Squeals.*

Grabbing the heavy cotton curtain, I yanked it open. Luz looked up, holding a wax strip covered in thick, dark hairs. On the other side of the waxing bed, my girlfriend held down a woman who was naked from the waist down, flat on her back, legs splayed. Luz stared at me. Billie stared at me. I stared from a stranger's face to her wide-open vagina. She stared at me, too.

I didn't know what to do. There seemed to be noises behind me, like little mice scurrying around, but it wasn't mice. Nope. It was Sandra in stilettos. She strode in front of me from god-knows-where and pulled the curtain shut before spinning around to scowl. Her eyes were like little black beads. "Get out," she said.

How could I argue with that?

"Here," Soo Jin said, taking the sushi from my hand. "I'll give Billie her lunch when she's done, okay?"

I left Billie's food with the pretty receptionist and raced to the door in a daze. When I got home, I turned the radio on, fell into my ugly chair, and stared out the window. I'd never felt so sheepish or so shaken.

Without looking at the clock, I couldn't tell if an hour or five minutes had gone by before Billie stormed through my front door. She was holding the sushi. That was a good sign, at least.

"Do you want me to lose my job?" she asked, slamming the sushi down on my table. Billie was beautiful when she was angry, but I wouldn't tell her that in the moment. Her pale cheeks filled with colour as she cried, "Sandra is livid. She holds me responsible for your actions."

I took a deep breath. "Sorry."

"Sorry's well and good until I get fired and no other salon will take me!"

How could I argue? She was right. I came off as a total sleaze and there was no way around it.

"I didn't know you were waxing," I said. "You're always on mani-pedi. I had no idea you even knew how to wax."

Billie shook her head, sighing. She picked up the sushi from the table and said, "Luz has been teaching me."

"That's cool." I moved my feet so she could sit on the footstool in front of me. "For how long now?"

Opening the plastic sushi case, Billie plucked out chopsticks and broke them apart. "A couple weeks."

It seemed a little strange that she'd spent weeks learning a new trade and didn't even mention it. I didn't want to come off as a possessive douche bag, but I had to ask, "Why didn't you say anything? That's big news. It's more money, right?"

"Yeah," Billie said. Her blood-red lips trembled as she stared into her sushi. Her cat's eyes grew puffy and red. I wanted to kiss every inch of her face. Even in silence, she looked mournfully beautiful, with her black rockabilly hair all pinned up under a retro lace veil. "I just..."

When the tears came, I took the sushi from her lap, picked her up, and placed her in mine. She threw her arms around my neck and cried against my shoulder. I hugged her hips, gently patting her bottom. "It's okay, babe. Tell me what's up."

She wiped her face on my T-shirt, which was fine because it was dirty anyway. With mucous still dripping from her nose and tears from her eyes, she said, "It's not you."

"Is this the old *it's not you, it's me*?" As soon as the words were out of my mouth, though, I panicked a bit. Maybe it was.

To my delight, she laughed through the tears. "It's not you, it's Allison."

My heart sank in my chest. "Who's Allison?"

"A girl I dated for a while." Billie shifted in my lap, leaning her head against my dry and unsnotty shoulder. "She said I was beautiful, but I'd be *more* beautiful if I wore the outfits she liked, the colours she liked, the make-up she liked. It all seemed harmless in the beginning, just little changes to make her happy. One day I woke up and realized I had no space for myself. She told me what to wear. She told me how to do my hair. 'You're not going out like that. You look like a five-dollar whore.' She'd manipulated me into allowing her to control my life. It was terrible."

I wondered why Billie hadn't told me this before, but that wasn't important, was it? She was telling me now.

"But she's out of your life and I'm in it," I said, trying to be uplifting. "And I think you're beautiful all the time. You're the most beautiful girl I've ever seen."

She really was.

Billie didn't seem to hear my compliments. "I have all these fears, Claire. They're not about you, but I put them on you. See what I mean?"

I was a dumb guy sometimes. "Not really."

She slumped down until her ear was against my chest. "I can hear your heartbeat," she said with a forlorn smile in her voice. "It's nice."

"Billie, bunny…" I would have kissed her forehead if it weren't for that damn veil. It was pretty, though. And it suited her. "You're being evasive."

Not that I could criticise. I did the same thing at times.

"I worry this will turn into that," she said. "I worry you'll be like her. I know you're not, but..."

"You don't trust me," I finished, making very sure that was a statement and not a question. I knew other women, and men too, who'd been in relationships like Billie's. They had a wounding effect on the psyche. I wouldn't let myself feel insulted. "That's okay. Trust takes time. We'll get there."

She hugged me tight and smiled. "I'm sorry I didn't tell you about the waxing. That would have been a no-no in Allison's books. Me around naked pussies? No way. I thought you'd be jealous."

"Well, I am a little jealous," I teased. "You get to play with pussies all day? That's what I call the sweet life."

With a giggle, she replied, "I get to *torture* pussies all day. It's not the same thing."

"Hey, whatever floats your boat."

It was a relief to see her smile as she stood up to fetch her sushi. Parking herself on the footstool, she dug into lunch like a hungry peasant. As she ate, it occurred to me that when I tore open that curtain, I *had* done it out of jealousy. I thought she was in there messing around with someone. That thought made me angry and resentful. It was hard to confess a thing like that, especially with Billie in such a fragile frame of mind, so I kept it to myself.

"Have you ever had a bikini wax?" she asked as she ate.

I laughed. "Do I look like someone who gets waxed?"

With a shrug, she said, "I don't know. You got a pedicure once."

"From you," I added as she lifted a piece of sushi to her mouth. "I just wanted to meet you. Every time I tried to say hi on the street, I chickened out. I get nervous talking to beautiful girls."

Billie smiled as she chewed. "Want one?"

I waved the sushi away. "Nah, I already ate, but thanks."

She leaned forward to kiss my cheek. "Not sushi, sweets. A bikini wax. Want one?"

Without meaning to, I laughed out loud. There were so many reasons to say no that I didn't know where to begin. "What, you mean at the salon? Because I'm pretty sure your boss just banned me for life."

"We could do it afterhours," she said with a sneaky grin. "I'm a key-holder now."

What other excuses could I come up with? "I've heard it hurts like hell."

"Oh, don't give me that." She spread some wasabi on her sushi and topped it with pickled ginger. "You have how many tattoos? I think you can handle a little hot wax."

She sure wasn't making it easy for me to resist the call of the wax. I tried to think up a better excuse than, "I'm a pussy and I can't take the pain," but it wasn't happening.

"Besides," she went on, "I think you'd taste great bare. And—who knows?—you might just enjoy the process."

Rising from the footstool, she pulled down on the hem of her black cotton dress. There was one last piece of sushi left in the plastic box, and I stared at it in displaced awe.

After tiptoeing to the door, Billie turned around and said, "Come down afterhours. We'll have a good time."

I nodded and said something completely incoherent. Billie had gone from crying to calm to flirty all in the space of one lunch hour. I hoped she was okay. I hoped she wasn't just putting kink on the table as an apology for being upset. Billie wasn't always the easiest girl to read.

But I would go. Of course I would. Billie was my girlfriend and I cared for her. Even if this little adventure hurt like hell, at least it would pay off in oral sex.

I am such a sleaze...

AS I SLIPPED DOWNSTAIRS, I couldn't stop thinking of the night I'd worked up the courage to introduce myself to Billie. I could see the salon from my apartment window and I knew she closed up shop alone on Wednesdays. It's not that I was stalking her or anything. Just watching.

She was the most gorgeous creature I'd ever seen. How could I look away?

The salon was locked, but when I tapped on the glass, Soo Jin answered.

"Come on in," she said with a smile.

"Oh, hi Soo Jin. I thought everyone would be gone by now." Meaning, *I thought you would be gone by now*.

"They are," she said, speeding away in those gorgeous black boots. They were so sexy I could have licked them. "Billie's ready for you. She asked me to stick around, but only if you don't mind."

Mind?

"No," I said, gazing at her lovely little body in that black cotton dress. "For sure stay."

Kiss me, suck me, lick me...

If Billie invited another girl to get in on the fun, it was all good in my books. I felt proud of her. That showed confidence and trust in our relationship. After the conversation we'd had just hours earlier, it seemed a whirlwind conversion.

The lights were dim when we arrived at the back corner of the salon. As Soo Jin pulled open the cotton curtain, ambient music spilled out from behind it. Billie had lit candles all around. A water fountain spilled a small stream over tumbled rocks. And there was Billie in her hot pink shoes and her black button-up dress. She took my breath away, and my vocabulary along with it.

Billie had touched up her make-up since lunchtime. Her black cat's eyes and purple shadow made her look a little like a Bond girl. And that red lipstick! God, it made my clit throb. I wanted to feel her lips on my pussy right away, but I suppose they'd be my prize for enduring the wax.

"I asked Soo Jin to stay," Billie told me.

"She mentioned that, yeah."

With a playful smirk, Billie undid the top two buttons of her dress. My pussy swelled as her grin grew. She unbuttoned the next one. Her tits sat in a bright red bra like two little white melons. I wanted to dive right in, even with Soo Jin standing next to me.

"Here. Take this." Billie handed me a glass of water and a liquid blue pill. "And then we'll get you undressed and up on the table."

"You don't have to drug me to get me in bed," I said.

Unbuttoning her skirt, Billie revealed her black thigh-high stockings to me. "It's just ibuprofen, silly. It'll take the edge off when we start ripping the hair from your flesh."

While Soo Jin gazed unapologetically at Billie's thighs, arousal sizzled on the air like fireworks ready to burst.

Strangely, Soo Jin's lusty looks didn't make me jealous in the least.

Interesting.

"Take off your pants," Billie said with a virginal smile.

Who was I to argue? I unlaced my boots, took off my socks, and dropped my pants. I was about to toss off my boyshorts when a wave of embarrassment overtook me. Sure, Billie had seen me in all states of attire, but what would Soo Jin make of my naked body?

"I can leave if you want," Soo Jin offered.

When she bit her lip, I felt bold. Tearing out of my underwear, I stood before my girlfriend and her fellow spa worker like a superhero.

"Stay," I said, and ripped off my T-shirt.

Billie giggled. "You didn't have to take your top off. We're only doing your bikini line."

"No, this is good." Soo Jin stepped close and stared—literally stared!—at my boobs. Then she said, "I can tweeze those hairs around your nipples, if you want."

Oh, for Christ's sake!

I was so mortified I collapsed on the waxing bed. I felt naked and under observation, like the Neanderthal getting checked out by the pretty scientists.

Billie stepped up to bat. Running her hands across my thighs, she said, "You look great, sweets. And when we're through with you, you're going to look amazing."

The adoration in Billie's eyes melted my humiliation. She had a way of setting my mind at ease, no matter the situation. That's one reason I loved her so much.

"Scooch up the table," Soo Jin told me. To Billie, she said, "You're lucky. Her hair's the perfect length for waxing. We won't have to trim it or anything."

I looked at Billie. "That *is* lucky."

"Well, Soo Jin knows more about this stuff than I do. She used to do waxing." Billie spoke quickly, like she didn't want me asking any questions. "Anyway, I'm going to start now by applying a hot compress to your pussy." She picked a wet cloth out of a steaming ceramic dish and wrung it out. "You ready for this?"

I wriggled with excitement. "Oh yeah."

When she pressed the hot cloth to my mound, my whole body heated up. With a cunning grin, Billie pushed her palm against my clit and moved it in slow circles. I let out a low moan. The heat and the pressure and the women in black made me crazy with the anticipation. I knew what was coming.

As Billie stroked my pussy with the hot cloth, Soo Jin stared down at my naked body. My tits swelled, feeling huge as my nipples hardened before our three sets of eyes. Billie licked her lips.

But it wasn't Billie who pounced.

Soo Jin dove at my breasts, pressing them together as she sucked the nearest nipple. That sensation of her warm, wet tongue flicking my flesh was so tremendous I grabbed the back of her neck and sent my fingers through her silky hair. When it released a lush tropical scent, the multiplicity of sensation was more than I could handle. I threw my head back and gave her a big moan.

All I wanted was to watch Soo Jin suck my tits, but my eyes kept rolling back. When I finally managed to fix on the world around me, my girlfriend's expression gripped me violently.

Billie.

She stood by me, staring at the pink traces of lipstick all over my chest. Her jaw tightened, but she didn't move. If I were to guess, I would have said she was in shock.

"What are you doing?" Billie asked. Her voice sounded small and hurt.

My stomach sunk as Soo Jin gazed up at my girlfriend. I didn't know what to say, but I gave it a shot. "I thought you wanted this."

"Yeah," Soo Jin chimed in, her voice high and wavering.

"No." Billie lifted the cloth from my mound and placed it in the ceramic bowl, seeming oddly disconnected from our scene. "Soo Jin has done this before. I just wanted her help. It's my first time."

My whole body went stiff. Billie was a waxing virgin? And she was about to tear the hair from my sensitive nether regions? "I thought you said Luz was training you."

"Yeah..." Now Billie was getting shifty—I could see it in her unbalanced motions. "Well, I help her by holding the ladies' legs down once in a while. You should see how some of them flail around like fish out of water."

When Billie's nervous chuckles trailed off, we were left with ambient music and the tinkle of the water fountain.

Soo Jin broke the silence, bursting with giggles. "Let me get this straight: you convinced Claire you knew what you were doing when she's really just your test subject? And here I thought you wanted to spice things up with a threesome! You really just asked me to here for guidance?"

"You told me you've been doing this for weeks!" I cried, unable to fathom why Billie would mislead me.

A stray smirk broke across her bright red lips. "Well, you were prepared to cheat on me."

"It's not cheating if you're standing there watching."

Soo Jin leaned against the waxing bed, tapping her fingers on the cushion. "Sounds like you two have trust issues. You should work on that... right after we finish this wax job."

I had to laugh. "Yes, Mother."

Rolling her eyes, Soo Jin said, "The next step is pre-epilation oil. Billie, I think you've got that covered."

"Oh. Yes." My girl sprang into action, pouring oil into her palm and then dripping it into my pubic hair. When her hand touched my mound, I nearly leapt from the table.

"How does that feel?" Billie cooed.

"Nice." It felt better than nice, actually, when she dipped into the curve of my thighs. "Oh wow. Let's just do this all night."

"Do you mind if I fondle your girlfriend's boobs?" Soo Jin asked Billie. And the guilt trip went on. "I *am* doing you a favour, staying late to help."

"Oh, go ahead. It's not cheating if I'm standing right here, *apparently*..." When Billie she pressed my hairy lips together, I knew all was well with the world. "Do you think that painkiller's kicked in yet?"

"Hehe. I don't know. Give me some pain and we'll find out." I crossed my arms behind my head, and the moment they were out of the way, Soo Jin grabbed my tits. Grabbed them, and squeezed. "Holy Mother! I don't know if it's the painkillers, but I'm feeling pretty good right now."

"Then it's time to get started," Soo Jin chimed in. "Billie's going to apply the hot wax, starting on the outer edges."

"Right." When Billie didn't move, I got nervous.

Soo Jin must have sensed my anxiety, because she worked her hands to my nipples and squeezed. "Billie, get your muslin strip ready."

I closed my eyes. I didn't want to see what was going on. In fact, a set of headphones would have been nice. Then I wouldn't have been able to hear Soo Jin gently scolding my girlfriend as she did everything wrong.

Leaning close, Soo Jin licked my nipples. That tongue was magic. She blew cool air on my tits just as Billie came in with the wax. It felt like hot honey spreading through my pubic hair and down my inner thighs. I understood food fetishists a little better as hot wax spread across my skin, making me wet.

"Now put the muslin on top and press down," Soo Jin instructed.

Billie did as she was told, applying pressure to the strip of fabric. "Is it okay, Claire?"

"Oh yeah!" I moaned as Soo Jin led her hot tongue across my chest. "I'm feeling pretty good right now, I gotta say."

With a smirk that could have been mistaken for cruel, Billie said, "Good."

Soo Jin turned toward Billie and her silky hair splashed across my chest. Billie raised a conspiring eyebrow as her co-worker said, "Remember to slap her. Slap her hard. It's got to be *hard*."

"Who, me?" I asked.

When they didn't answer, I knew it had to be me who was about to get smacked... *hard*.

"Do you think it's ready to come off now?" Billie asked Soo Jin.

Backing away, Soo Jin said, "Give it thirty seconds. Come kiss your girlfriend while you wait."

I knew how much Billie hated smearing her lipstick when other people were around, but she lunged at me nonetheless. Her tongue shocked mine—warm and strong, teasing. I reached around the back of her neck, pulling her close until I felt her chest on my bare tits.

My pussy begged for Soo Jin, and she didn't waste time getting all up in there. Her little fingers tickled my flesh inside and out. They were a perfect complement to my Billie's hard kisses. Soo Jin made me smile inwardly—one of those girls who couldn't resist the call of a wet pussy. She came, she saw, she fingerfucked.

I acted experienced around my girlfriend, but I'd never actually been with two girls at the same time. It was all a macho act, pretending I'd done everything there was to do in the world of lesbian sex. And I'd certainly never been waxed, but Billie already knew that.

"You do the first one," Billie begged Soo Jin. "Show me how it's done."

"If you insist." Soo Jin grabbed the muslin strip adhered to my crotch. "Watch closely. I'm going to tear it off fast, then give her a good whack. You ready, Claire?"

"Yeah." I was strong like bull. I could handle anything.

Except waxing.

When Soo Jin tore off the wax strip, I howled. "Jesus motherfucker Mary and Virgin *fuck*!"

My flesh blazed, and Soo Jin's solution was to smack it with her pussy-wetted hand. *Slap, slap, slap* right against my inner thigh and my mound. It felt strangely wonderful and it hurt like hell. My tough butch exterior melted as I choked back tears.

"When Luz waxes, presses down on the skin." Leaning over my naked body, Billie showed Soo Jin what she meant. Her hand soothed my sizzling skin just by being there. "I'll do the next one, okay?"

Soo Jin slid out of the way so Billie could drizzle hot wax down the other side of my pussy. With a wooden applicator, she spread the warm stuff around my mound and down my thigh. Soo Jin traced her fingernails around my belly, and I reached for her hand to hold as Billie pressed on the muslin strip.

"Can I squeeze your hands?" I asked.

"Of course," she said. "Just don't break any bones. I have a suspicion you could."

Billie chimed in. "I'm going to give your puss a rubdown while we're waiting."

Her red lipstick was smudged from kissing. It was probably all over me, too. When she eased her knuckles in against my clit, I gasped. My girlfriend's touch affected me so deeply I smiled through the lingering burn.

"Do you do this for all your clients?" I asked. "Or am I special?"

Kneading my pussy with her knuckles, Billie said, "You know you are. You're the best thing that's ever happened to me."

Without warning, she grabbed the muslin and pulled it off quick like a bandage.

I was too surprised even to scream, but Soo Jin hollered for me while I squeezed the hell out of her hand. "Fuck, Claire! You're killing me, here."

"Sorry," I said as Billie laid a few temperate slaps against my flesh.

"You've got to do it harder," Soo Jin said. "Let me do it."

Stealing her hands away from mine, she slapped my mound so hard my skin glowed bright red. Shots of pain razed me, running down my legs like little explosions. Fire ignited all over me, over my skin and inside my veins. But, damn, it felt good to be whacked by the girls. I'd never been one for spankings, but after this I might have to be naughty every so often just to incur Billie's punishing palm.

Billie and Soo Jin leaned over my body from opposite sides of the waxing bed. They whispered back and forth, their lips grazing each other's cheeks and ears as they spoke.

"What are you two conspiring about?" I asked. Not that I was suspicious or anything.

With a wide grin, Billie said, "For our next act, we're going to double up on you."

I gulped. "What does that mean?"

"I'm going to wax," Billie replied.

"And I'm going to slap," Soo Jin said.

How could I argue? Soo Jin was by far the better slapper.

As Billie heaped on the hot stuff, I asked Soo Jin, "Why don't you wax anymore? You're so good at it."

Billie looked up as she spread wax along the landing strip in the middle of my mound. It was all coming off. Every hair must go.

"I had a client once," Soo Jin confessed. "Said she was an actress. She was shooting a movie and she needed to be all clean down there."

Billie placed a muslin strip on the wax and pressed. Was it just my imagination, or could I feel its heat on my clit?

"So, you know what I'm thinking?" Soo Jin asked. "*Porn*. Right? She was gorgeous."

Billie chuckled. "She was gorgeous, so obviously she was a porn star."

Rolling her eyes, Soo Jin said, "Anyway, this girl takes off her skirt and her panties, and I'm thinking, *She'll be cool. This is what she does for a living.* So I plunge my face between her legs and start eating her."

"What?" I arched up from the waxing bed, but Billie pushed me back down. "You really did that? Without warning?"

"I couldn't resist," Soo Jin said. "But I should have, because she pushed my head away, screaming, like, 'What the fuck?' That girl was livid. She complained to Sandra and it turned into this whole big thing. Apparently she was shooting a feature film, not porn. I was lucky Sandra didn't fire me. Now I'm just not allowed to have physical contact with clients."

Before I could say anything, Billie tore the muslin from my mound, ripping stubborn hair from my flesh. This sting was even worse than before—a blinding agony that made me dizzy. More than dizzy. Waves of nausea turned my belly like a tumble dryer, and it didn't help much when Soo Jin slapped my blazing skin.

"Jesus-fucking-Christ!" I cried. "You could have given me some warning."

"It's better not to," Billie said as Soo Jin smacked my cunt. "I don't want you worrying yourself into a tizzy."

"*Tizzy*," Soo Jin repeated. "That's a funny word."

Billie leaned in, stopping just short of my lips. "I love you, Claire-Bear."

"You've got a funny way of showing it, ripping all the hair from my body."

I kissed my girl while Soo Jin went ape on my mound. That woman pummelled me with an open palm, sending resounding smacks into the air, one after another after another. My pussy stung like fuck, but Soo Jin's slap-slap-slap made me feel a little better, strangely, and Billie's eat-me kisses took me everywhere.

When Billie backed away, Soo Jin stopped spanking me. Everything pulsed—my outer skin, my thighs, my slick inner lips. It throbbed like a second heartbeat.

"I love you too," I told my girl, reaching for her hand. "You are beautiful, you know."

She blushed, covering her smudged lipstick.

Intruding on our moment, Soo Jin said, "If you two had trust issues, they should all be cleared up now."

"What do you mean?" I asked.

She pressed both hands on my mound and I nearly jumped out of my skin. "Well, Billie, Claire got felt up by another girl and she still loves you better than anything. Claire, you gave Billie the benefit of the doubt and agreed to let her rip all the hair from your pussy."

I laughed. "Yeah, I guess that does require trust."

"We're not finished yet," Billie said. "Close your eyes, Claire. I'm going to trim you up while Soo Jin gets those hairs from around your nipples."

I'd hoped they wouldn't mention those again...

"And then we'll treat you to a little after-wax massage," Soo Jin went on.

I did as instructed, lying back with my eyes closed. Soothing music twinkled on the evening air. The space smelled like vanilla and chai from all the scented candles. The girls were quiet as they went to work, Billie trimming the hairs from my lips with tiny scissors as Soo Jin plucked my tits. After the torture they'd put me through, taking out those hairs barely felt like a pinprick.

When she was done, Soo Jin licked circles around my nipples with the tip of her tongue. Billie wrung out her warm cloth and placed it on my mound. I don't think I'd ever been so wet in all my life.

As Soo Jin sucked my nipples, Billie stroked her post-epilation lotion all over my searing pussy. It felt so good to hurt so bad, especially with two dark-haired beauties in black cotton dresses taking good care of me.

Billie rubbed my thighs. She worked her way to my hairless pussy lips, pressing them against each other and rubbing back and forth. As she pushed that tender flesh in opposite directions, it gently stroked my clit from the outside in. She cupped my mound with both hands and used her palms to press. The constant motion on my clit made me tremble. That girl really knew how to get me off.

I ran my hand through Soo Jin's hair and she shot me a smile as she switched tits. Getting suckled was heaven on earth, and I felt it in my clit as Billie slipped her finger between my slick lips. My wetness started dripping from my slit and down my asshole. I felt slippery all over.

Billie moved her palms faster, up and down, in syncopated rhythms. I sang her praises. Oh yes. She was that good.

"Billie, girl, go faster. Make me come. I'm so close, babe."

Soo Jin bit my nipple as Billie's palm raced against my pussy. The girls were so good to me. My clit throbbed and my toes tingled. I could barely keep still. They held me down and worked me hard while I writhed against the waxing bed.

Billie didn't let go of my blazing pussy lips. She held them between her palms, just held them, and the lack of external motion made my body jump inside itself. My clit begged for a rub. It jerked itself off, leaping inside my juicy lips like a pearl between two hot, wet oyster shells. I came again, enclosed in my girl's hands, with Soo Jin's soft tongue still working my tits.

"Oh Billie," I chanted. "Oh babe. Oh my god!"

Panting hard, I opened my eyes to see two beautiful girls smiling back at me.

"How did you like that?" Billie asked.

I laughed. "You really have to ask?"

With a generous smile, Soo Jin started cleaning the mess they'd made. Billie picked up a mirror and held it between my legs. "What do you think?"

My skin was still pink and puffy, but my pussy looked so clean and fresh I wished I could eat myself. Which reminded me... "Wasn't I promised a little lip service to go with this bikini wax?"

Billie let out a lilting giggle. "How about I let your pretty little pussy recover before I destroy it again?"

I couldn't argue with that logic. Leaning forward, I planted an exhausted kiss on my girlfriend's lipstickless lips.

"Thanks," I said, grabbing Soo Jin's hand. "You two sure know how to turn a butch dyke into a trembling pussy."

Popcorn

Eddie has the craziest fantasies, and somehow he always manages to draw me into them.

On the way home from another excruciating office party, my crazy boyfriend started teasing me about how affectionate I am with two of my co-workers. I'd never really thought about it, but Sharmini and I always have our arms around each other's waists, and Dulce-Maria can't get through an entire conversation without petting my arm or my belly. I guess Eddie's right—we're an affectionate bunch.

"It's more than just affectionate," Eddie disputed in the car as we drove home from my office. "They want you!"

"They do not!" I scoffed, chuckling at the thought. "You're such an idiot, sweety."

That's when my mind started to wander. Sure, I'd noticed they're attractive girls, but I'd never considered how sexy they really are. Sharmini is shorter than I am, with plump cheeks, long wavy hair, and luscious curves. Dulce-Maria is taller-than-tall in the stiletto pumps she always wears, and her hair is jet black like Sharmini's, but always expertly coiffed. "Fashionista" describes her to a T.

"What did you say you were you craving at the party?" Eddie asked, interrupting my reverie. I smirked. "To eat, I mean. Remember what you said?"

"Popcorn." That's what I'd been craving. He'd poured me a glass of red wine, and there's something about a nice merlot that makes me desperate for popcorn.

"A whole tub of it," Eddie continued. "And the whole time I watched you chatting with your girlfriends, all I could imagine was you, Sharmini, and Dulce-Maria in a great big hot tub full of popcorn."

I laughed my ass off at the idea of a hot tub full of anything right in the middle of my office, but the more I processed Eddie's insane conception, the hotter it got me. I imagined booting all our coworkers out and starting a party of our own. We would giggle at first, the three of us, like this was the silliest thing we'd ever done.

Dulce-Maria would strip off her designer dress and what would be underneath? Lovely, lacy lingerie, of course. Her gorgeous tits would flow out overtop her firm designer bra, and the line of her legs and her ass would be undeniably feminine in those high-heeled shoes.

Sharmini would tear off her special-occasion sari, and underneath she'd be completely nude. Her bare breasts would bounce as she tossed the sari over her shoulder and begin her seductive approach. Those cinnamon fingers would unzip my little red dress, letting it fall to the floor, and I'd step out of it with my wine glass still in hand.

Releasing the clasp on my bra and shifting out my panties, I would laugh as I climbed into the huge tub of warm, freshly-popped corn. I'd sink down into it, with Sharmini at my side, and we'd splash each other. I'd still be digging popcorn out of my red wine as Dulce-Maria came over with a gravy boat full of liquid butter. I'd shoot her one of those looks that says,

"You wouldn't dare!" but she would do it anyway, pouring the melted butter all over me.

With a risqué giggle, Sharmini would smooth the butter all down my chest, rubbing it into my breasts and my belly. When she splashed me again, the light-as-air popcorn would stick to my boobs. Dulce-Maria would toss off her heels and sink into the tub to sprinkle me with salt before the two of them bowed their heads and started eating.

Dulce-Maria would work her way up my belly, lifting each piece of popcorn off me with the tip of her tongue. Sharmini would shoot straight for my breasts, devouring the popcorn first and my flesh second. She'd lick the salt from my skin and suck the butter from my nipples while Dulce-Maria ran her tongue up my neck. I'd close my eyes and she'd kiss me with those fiery red lips.

Amidst the passion of that kiss, Dulce-Maria would reach down between my thighs. She'd find my pussy with her fingers while Sharmini sucked away at my tits, pausing every so often to snack on the popcorn sticking to my buttery flesh. I would melt into their arms as Dulce-Maria pierced my slit with her long fingers, coating my clit in pussy juice. She'd rub me in quick, frenzied motions while she and Sharmini planted hot kisses along my neck. The faster she stroked me, the louder I'd get, until I was crying out in the ecstasy of the moment.

As I panted, trying desperately to catch my breath, my girlfriends would blow cool air across my sizzling skin. When I came back down to earth, we'd pour ourselves another glass of wine and snack on popcorn while we giggled about the crazy thing we'd just done.

"What are you thinking about?" Eddie asked me as we pulled into the front drive.

I just smirked at him and shrugged. "Popcorn."

You might also enjoy:

Sapphic Confessions
24 Kinky Lesbian Sex Stories
By Giselle Renarde

I KISSED A GIRL... and I didn't stop there!

Twenty-four eye-opening lesbian tales so titillating you won't be able to resist reading the next confession. Butches, femmes, chapstick lesbians, bisexual beauties, experienced older women and curious first-timers admit to their naughty deeds in this hot new short story collection.

Bad girls get caught being naughty in church.

A bi femme gets spanked by a butch stranger in her pool's sauna room.

An established couple hires a gorgeous girl for a first-time threesome.

A fiery motorcycle dyke makes a scene outside a lesbian nightclub.

An incorrigible house painter converts rich MILFs in their own homes.

Driving lessons get dirty on a dusty country road.

All this and so much more in Sapphic Confessions: 24 Kinky Lesbian Sex Stories!

Giselle Renarde's erotic fiction has appeared in over 100 anthologies, including prestigious collections like Best Lesbian Erotica, Best Lesbian Romance, Best Women's Erotica, Girl Fever, and the Lambda Award-winning collection Wild Girls, Wild Nights.

ABOUT THE AUTHOR

Giselle Renarde is an award-winning queer Canadian writer. Nominated Toronto's Best Author in NOW Magazine's 2015 Readers' Choice Awards, her fiction has appeared in well over 100 short story anthologies, including prestigious collections like Best Lesbian Romance, Best Women's Erotica, and the Lambda Award-winning collection Take Me There, edited by Tristan Taormino. Giselle's juicy novels include Anonymous, Cherry, Seven Kisses, The Other Side of Ruth, the Lesbian Diaries series, and the Wedding Heat series.

Giselle Renarde
Canada just got hotter!
Want to stay up to date? Visit
http://donutsdesires.blogspot.com[1]!
Sign up for Giselle's newsletter: http://eepurl.com/R4b11
Weekly Audio Erotica at http://Patreon.com/AudioErotica

---

1. http://donutsdesires.blogspot.com/

2

Milton Keynes UK
Ingram Content Group UK Ltd.
UKHW020734040823
426331UK00014B/492